THE BIG GAMBLE

M. ANDREWS

The Big Gamble
Gambling on Love Series Book One
M. Andrews

ISBN—13: 987-1517605971
ISBN—10: 1517605970

Editing by:
Payne Proof

Cover design by:
Kari March Designs
Cover image copyright 2016

Formatting by:
Perfectly Publishable

DEDICATION

This is for all the people who have
taken a gamble on love and won.

PROLOGUE

Brooke

THE BEADS OF RAIN TRICKLED down my bedroom window as I watched the world below me, slowly realizing this would be the last time I'd look out at the New York skyline I called home. Fitting how today it was raining, something I'd need to get used to now that I was moving to one of the rainiest cities in the country, Seattle.

"Are you sure you want to do this?" I looked up spotting my big brother Hunter's reflection in the glass. "You could always move in with me if it's just a change of scenery that you're looking for."

Hunter was sweet to offer, but as much as I would love to move to Brooklyn, it wasn't going to help me feel any better.

"I wish it were that easy Hunter. I can't go anywhere in this city without it sparking some memory of Jake and me. And it's killing me."

My fiancé, Jake, passed away two years ago. We'd met three years before that when I was still *finding* myself. I'd moved to New York after dropping out of Harvard Medical School. I had big dreams of becoming a doctor when I was a kid, but once I got into the program I quickly realized being a doctor wasn't for me. So I hopped on a train to New York to find myself. I was working at one of the three jobs I maintained to keep myself afloat—a barista in a coffee shop in the financial district—when Jake walked in. He was handsome and charming and he had me the moment his fingers grazed my hand as I was handing him his coffee.

Our relationship was a whirlwind of lavish parties and private jets to Paris and Milan. He introduced me to a world that a girl raised by a single dad, who worked as a police detective, could only have dreamt about. Besides showing me how the other half lived, he also helped me find who I really was. I'd always had a secret dream of becoming a writer, but it had been drilled into my head by my grandmother that I had to grow up and get a real job, like being a doctor. But the idea of writing books and giving the stories that were always rolling around in my head a voice still haunted me. After meeting Jake, my muse was awakened, and I found my voice. And Jake gave me the support I needed to pursue my dream.

For three years, we were so happy. I wrote my books and started making a name for myself, while Jake became a wolf on Wall Street. We had everything. That was until that fateful day when one phone call threw my world on its head.

As soon as I woke up that morning, I was plagued with an uneasy feeling, like something was off, and it only got worse after Jake left for his morning run. I paced through our apartment trying to shake this feeling that was now like a bowling ball in the pit of my stomach.

Did I forget to pay a bill? Did I miss a deadline?

I ran through my entire schedule. Even tried yoga, but nothing was helping. By the time seven-thirty rolled around and Jake still hadn't returned from his run, I started to panic.

Jake was a creature of habit, rarely ever straying too far from his daily routine. Up and out the door by five for his run then home and making love to me in the shower by six. So I knew something wasn't right. When my phone rang at eight, I didn't have to answer it to know something had happened to Jake. The nurse on the other line tried her best to convince me that Jake was going to be just fine, he was in the hands of the best neurosurgeon in the country. I'd gone through enough medical training in med school to know that a ruptured aneurysm was a death sentence.

The moment I saw the sympathetic look in the doctor's eyes when I arrived at the hospital, I knew Jake was gone. He explained that he did everything in his power to stop the bleeding but the rupture was too big, and Jake had passed away on the operating table.

A part of me died with Jake that day, and now all I feel is numb and hollow. My feeling of emptiness only growing worse by me staying in New York, which is why I've decided to move to Seattle for a change of scenery and a fresh start.

"It just feels like you are running away again," Hunter added, while he leaned up against the doorway, arms folded in front of his chest.

I wouldn't have survived all of this it wasn't for Hunter. After the funeral, he took a leave of absence from his job as a photojournalist to take care of me. He kept me from sliding deep into the depths of hell. For which, I will never be able to pay him back.

"When I left Boston I was running away but this time it feels like I am running toward something. That something is pulling me to go to Seattle. I have to at least try and see if this is the push I need to getting my life back on track," I replied, still staring out at the rain.

"I think I'm just being selfish. I've liked having you here in New York, knowing when I come home from an assignment you would be here." He stepped up behind me, spinning me around, and he pulled me into his arms. "I'm just going to miss you so damn much, Brookie."

"I'm going to miss you too, Hunter. I can't thank you enough for everything you've done for me. It really means a lot, more than you'll ever know." I buried my face in his chest, my tears soaking into his shirt. He hugged me tighter, strumming his fingers through my hair like he did when I was a kid after I'd had a nightmare. I softly cried as we stood in my empty apartment. Hunter and my dad were all the family I had left, and it pained me to move so far away from them. But I needed this, I needed a fresh start. I couldn't spend my life living in the past anymore. It was time for me to start living again.

CHAPTER ONE

Brooke

Nine Months Later

A GENTLE BREEZE BLOWS IN through my bedroom window, making the sheer white linen curtains dance along the wall by my desk. The afternoon sun is breaking through the gray clouds hanging low on the Seattle skyline. I should be outside enjoying this rare beautiful fall day. Instead I'm stuck behind my desk, staring at a blank computer screen. The flashing cursor is taunting me, reminding me of what an epic failure I am.

I should be putting the final touches on my latest novel. Truth be told, this book should have been done over a year ago. After I killed off my characters in my last series, I haven't been able to write a single word. I've tried every trick in the book to get rid of my writers block, but nothing seems to be working.

I went as far as packing up my life and moving to a new city. I spent six months looking for the right apartment. I drove my realtor, Becky, crazy trying to find a place that felt like home. We searched every neighborhood in Seattle and still nothing gave me that vibe I was looking for. I was about to give up when Becky called saying she found a new listing that would be perfect for me in the Belltown neighborhood. It's two blocks from Pikes Place Market and, the part that got me to leave my room at the Fairmont . . . it over looked the Sound.

The moment I walked inside the Viktoria building, I started to feel the tingles of home. As I stepped off the elevator on the eighth floor the tingles turned into a full roar. When I ran my hand along the oak wood door I knew in an instant this was my new home. I didn't even care what the inside looked like, all I knew was that every nerve, every sense in my body, was telling me this was where I was supposed to be.

That was three months ago. Granted, I still love my new place with its exposed brick walls, beautiful dark oak wood floors, and the bay of windows that have the perfect view of the Seattle Great Wheel and the water. It still hasn't helped me with my writers block. I guess I was a fool to think any of this would work. But I can't fight the feeling that there is something more for me here. I just wish God or fate or whoever the hell brought me to Seattle would show their hand already.

I poured the last of my wine in my glass. Just as I set the bottle down on my desk I hear the faint opening guitar lick of Paradise City coming through my bedroom wall, signaling my new neighbor was home. This is one of my favorite Guns and Roses songs, so I can't help but to tap my foot to the beat and sway to the rhythm in my chair. I have to say, neighbor boy has great taste in music, it's also better than the sounds that usually come through his wall. Usually around three a.m. and usually some bimbo screaming about how amazing he and his cock are.

Nothing like being woken up out of a dead sleep to the sounds of "oh God, Brian, you're a god," or "oh God I love your cock!" to make you want to throat punch someone. I rarely sleep as it is, so what little sleep I do get, I don't interrupted by the blaring reminder that I'm not getting any.

In the middle of my air guitar solo my phone rings and, fuck me, it's my publisher, Michael. It's like he can sense that I'm procrastinating. I reluctantly answer the call. I've been avoiding Michael's calls and emails since I moved, over nine months ago.

Barrette Publishing is one of the top publishing houses in country. They took a chance on me and signed me over five years ago. We had a good relationship, I wrote them gold and made them a lot of money, so in return, they left me alone to work my magic. After Jake passed they gave me time to grieve. But I'm over a year late in turning in my new manuscript and they want it now.

"Hey Michael, I was just going to call you," I lie.

"Sure you were Miss McCoy." I cringe at his aggravated tone. "Now that I have your attention, Miss McCoy, I would like you to come down to my office tomorrow morning at ten to discuss your new book, or the lack thereof. It's imperative that you make it to this meeting."

I've been putting this day off for far too long, and now it's time I meet my maker. "I'll be there with bells on," I nervously joke.

"See you tomorrow, Miss McCoy," he says in an unamused tone before hanging up.

I drop my phone back on my desk and gulp back the rest of the red wine in my glass. My head drops to the hard wooden top of my desk as I gently pound my forehead in shame.

"I am so fucking screwed!"

CHAPTER
TWO

Brian

"YOU LOOKIN' FOR A LITTLE trouble, sweetheart?"

"Maybe." The shy redhead giggles. Her face is flush with nervous excitement as her eyes trail down my body. Her thighs clench together when she spots the bulge hiding behind my jeans. *I know you want to meet him, sweetheart.*

I lean in nice and close, resting my hands on the bar behind her, framing her petite body between my arms. "I think you are," I whisper in her ear. A sly smirk tugs at my lips when I hear her breathing grow ragged.

"Do you have a name to go along with that pretty face?"

Her cheeks burn an even brighter shade of red, making the freckles that dot her face pop. She introduces herself as Tiffany or Tara. Something with a T, but like it really matters. Red isn't going to be seeing much of me after tonight. And I know what you're thinking, but I make these women no promise other than to give them a night they will look back on, probably while in bed while their bloated, balding, Viagra-fueled husbands flop on top of them. As I see it, I'm doing these girls a great service while also taking care of my own needs.

"And what's your name handsome?" She softly giggles. She is so sweet and innocent it's almost painful.

"It's Brian," I reply

"Well Brian, just so you know, I've never done anything like this before." She pulls her lip nervously between her teeth and all I can think is how good her full ruby red lips will look wrapped around my cock.

"And what's that darlin'?" I breathe in her sweet cherry blossom scent, lips barely grazing the soft, creamy skin of her neck. I can't wait to get her back to my place and taste every inch of her body.

"Gone home with a guy I just met," she says in a breathy whisper.

I could believe that. The moment I saw her from across the bar I knew she wasn't like the rest of the badge bunnies that hangout at Murphy's. It's well known around Belltown that Murphy's Irish Pub is the cop hangout. Everyone down at the Second hits Murphy's to blow off some steam after a shift. It's dark, the floors are sticky, but the beer is cheap, and there are always plenty of hot girls in short skirts looking to hook up with anyone flashing a badge. It's not exactly the kind of place a little rich girl like Red would come to unless she was looking to piss off daddy. Red here probably has a boyfriend who only likes to fuck in the missionary position with all the lights off. I can smell her need for a good fuck all over her, and I'm more than happy to help.

"Let me show you how good it can be to be a little bad."

Her whole body shudders at the idea, and I can feel the heat radiating off of her. I know I have her right where I want her. She slides off her bar stool then struts over to where her friends are sitting to grab her bag. I wave at the group of giggling woman when they all look over at me. I have to stop myself from asking Red to bring along her hot friends, figuring coming home with me is about as adventurous as she is going to get.

Sliding my arm around her tiny waist, I lead us out of the

bar and down the two blocks to my apartment. As we step into the elevator and the doors close, an image of my ex, Jillian, flashes through my mind. Her bright auburn hair and wicked grin punching me in the gut, and I can't help but feel slightly sorry this chick is a redhead, but only a little. I guess I should feel bad for dicking these women over, but after having your heart ripped out by one it's hard to feel anything at all.

* * *

"Spank me, Daddy. I've been such a bad wittle girl."

Seriously, baby talk? Talk about a wood killer. Not that Red was doing that great of a job keeping me hard since we got back to my place. Don't get me wrong, she has a hot body, a tiny waist, and a decent pair of tits, but I prefer more curves on a girl. I like having something to grab onto. Between her small frame and her sloppy attempt at a blowjob, it was taking everything I had to keep it up.

As I reared my hand back, I could hear a loud pounding on my apartment door.

"Open up asshole, I know you're in there." A muffled woman's voice echoes through my apartment.

Red looks back at me with daggers in her eyes. "Is that your girlfriend?"

"Fuck no. I don't do girlfriends." It's three in the damn morning, who the fuck would have the balls to come knocking on my door at this hour? Then again, that blonde, stage five clinger I booted out of my place the other night might have cause for retaliation. I barely let her put her clothes on before I was shoving her out the door.

I climb out of bed, wrapping a sheet around my waist. The knocking growing louder and angrier as I walk through the living room to the front door.

"You gotta lot of fucking nerve . . ."

I fumble opening the locks and fling open the door. My mouth drops open and my anger quickly subsides when I spot the curvy brunette standing at my door. My eyes immediately focus on her body, making no attempt to hide the fact that I'm making a mental map of every curve of her banging figure. She's dressed in a tight pair of curve-hugging yoga pants and a see-through pink lace bra that barely contains her gorgeous full tits. Her perfect pink nipples standing at attention, almost saying, "Please come suck on us."

I finally meet her gaze, her big blue doe eyes hitting me right in the dick. I've only just seen her and she's already making me harder than Red had done all night. God damn, she's the most beautiful woman I've ever seen. She must be my new neighbor. I knew the place next door sold a few months ago, after Mrs. Perkins moved down to Arizona to live with her son. I hadn't seen who had moved in. Damn, had I known this beauty was living next door I would have introduced myself sooner and under better terms.

"So sweetheart, are you here to join the party?" I flash her a wink, but it only seems to piss her off even more.

"In your fucking dreams," she hisses. "Look, this is the third night in a row that you've kept me awake. I'm cool with you being a permanent stop for the skank train, but could you at least keep the noise down to a dull roar?"

I watch as her eyes dart from my mine down to my waist then back up to my face . . . then down again. Eyes widening when she notices how hard she's got me under the sheet. She stumbles over her words as she continues to rip me a new one about the noise.

"Just calm down darlin'. The noise can't be that bad."

"Not that bad . . . my ass. I almost got a concussion from one the pictures hanging above my bed crashing down on top of me."

I can't help but smile proudly about that statement. "I'm sorry for disturbing you, but we could have settled this in the morning. You didn't need to come over here banging on my door like a crazy person, trying to tell me what I can and cannot do in the privacy of my own home." Now I'm starting to get pissed off. Who's she to tell me what I could do in my own home? She doesn't see me coming over to her apartment at three in the damn morning screaming at her to keep the noise down. Oh wait, now I can see what this is really about.

"I don't give a shit what you do in your apartment. You can swing off the rafters for all I care, but what I do care about is when it keeps me from sleeping. Shove the bitches face in a pillow or strap a ball gag on her for all I care. Just keep the bitch fucking quiet!"

Ball gag, I like that one. Damn, one minute she's pissing me off then the next she's making me laugh. She's a fun one, I'll give her that. "I can see what's really got your panties in a twist. You're not mad about the noise. You're jealous that it's not you I'm banging into the wall." I take a step toward her, resting an arm on the door frame, I lean in close. "Do you want to take a ride on this train?"

An angry fire explodes in her eyes just before her hand cracks hard across my face. "Asshole," she screams, then storms off in a huff, slamming her door behind her.

"Crazy bitch." I rub my burning cheek and shut the door with a loud thud. That crazy bitch has some nerve, she's lucky I don't arrest her ass for assaulting a police officer. Red appears in the doorway of my bedroom, a concerned look painted across her face.

"Who was that?"

"Just my crazy bitch neighbor. Come on, we're moving the fun out here." I grab her arm and pull her over to the kitchen table, bending her over and spreading her legs wider with my knee. I pause for a moment when her fucking words ring in my head, "just keep the bitch quiet." What am I doing? Generally, I wouldn't give a shit what other people thought about what I'm doing but, here I am, going out of my way not to piss off some woman I don't even know.

Red looks back at me asking if I'm okay, and all I can see is that crazy bitch's face taunting me, those damn blue eyes burning into my soul. I take a step back. My eyes close tightly, trying to get her out of my head. I jump when I feel a hand sliding down my arm, it's Red asking me again if I'm okay. I open my mouth to speak and the only words that come out are, "Get the fuck out."

"What?" She cocks a puzzled eyebrow up at me.

"What part of get out don't you understand?" I bark callously.

"Please, Brian, let me stay. I can make you feel better." She reaches for me again, but I push her away. I can't deal with her right now.

"No, just get your shit and get out." I storm into my bedroom and pick up Red's clothes, tossing them at her. "I'm going to take a shower and when I get out you better not be here." I slam the bathroom door shut, hearing a muffled "You're an asshole" come through the door.

Tell me something I don't know, sweetheart.

I drop the sheet from around my waist and step into the shower, turning on the faucet, the cold water washing over me. I lean against the shower wall resting my head on the cold tiles. Closing my eyes, *her* face appears again. The first thing I see are her intense sapphire blue eyes . . . and her tits. God, I just want to live between them. And her lips, full and luscious, I just want to lick and bite at them. Next thing I know, I'm rock hard. No woman has had this type of effect on me in a long time, but why does it have to be her? My hand grips my cock, stroking slowly as I picture her on her knees in front of me, fucking me with that big mouth of hers. Looking up at me with those soul piercing eyes as I ram my dick down her throat. That will teach you to make demands of me, you crazy bitch.

"Oh fuck," I cry out, slamming my hand against the tile wall as I come in my other hand. My breathing stills and her image fades away. As my mind starts to clear, I realize she's the first woman not to fall for my usual charm. She pushed me away and, as much as I want to hate her, it only makes me want her more.

CHAPTER THREE

Brooke

"FUCK YOU SUN," I GROAN, peeling my eyes open. The bright morning light hitting me straight in the retinas.

Note to self—Buy curtains for the wall of windows I now hate.

I pull back the blankets and sit up from the couch. My muscles are sore from sleeping on the stiff cushions. After I stormed off from my altercation with the asshole, I crashed on my couch to avoid listening to him and his skank bang against my bedroom wall. When I first moved in the sexcapades had been few and far between. The past couple weeks it seems the asshole is on a mission to bang every woman in Seattle. And after three nights in a row of interrupted sleep, I snapped.

I stretch my arms above my head, flashes of the night's argument causing me to cringe. God, why did I have to go over there? I've never been one to think before I leap when I'm in full rage mode. A lack of sleep and stress about being behind on my new book definitely didn't help. A part of me felt awful for how I'd acted, and maybe the slap to his face was a bit dramatic, but a bigger part of me thought the cocky prick had it coming. Especially after he had the nerve to tell me I was jealous that it wasn't me he was fucking. So what that I haven't had sex in over two years, and that hearing his moans through my wall drenches my panties. Doesn't mean I want to fuck that asshole.

Well, maybe it does.

Getting up from the couch, I head to the bathroom, and that's when I catch a glimpse of myself in the mirror. My dark brown hair is a tangled mess, dark circles under my eyes and . . . oh my God! In my rage, I'd managed to put on pants, but neglected to put a shirt on. I look down at my sheer pink bra, my nipples on full display. That explains why he couldn't stop staring at my tits. Could this get any fucking worse?

I splash my face with some cold water and, as I do, an image of his lean muscular chest taunts me. The sweat glistening off his tanned muscles and that V, that fucking V. God help me, I wanted to run my tongue along every delicious inch of him and see what was hiding under that sheet. As the image plays in my mind, I feel a familiar ache between my thighs. My attention shifts down between my legs.

"Really? You couldn't do this for the sweet cute cop, Ryder, from the coffee shop? No. You have to come alive for that asshat next door. You're such a little bitch." You're losing it, Brooke. You're a grown ass woman yelling at your vagina. I splash more cold water on my face, trying to calm my now overheated body.

I slip out of my clothes and step into the shower. Turning on the water, the cold hits me like an icy wave making me squeal while my hands fumble with the knobs and finally finding the hot water. I stand under the spray letting the warmth wash over me. The moment I close my eyes . . . he's back . . . pressing me against the wall, pinning my wrists above my head in one of his strong hands while the other teases between my legs. Lips tasting my neck. I quickly turn off the hot water and let the cold water shock me back into reality. Get it together Brooke.

⋆ ⋆ ⋆

I emerge from my apartment an hour later feeling somewhat human. I managed to hide the dark circles under my eyes with a few coats of concealer and tamed my wild locks into a sleek ponytail. I'm dressed in my favorite pink pencil dress, black Louboutin heels, and a white trench coat. After an IV of coffee, I will be ready for my meeting with my publisher.

Stepping out of my apartment, I peer over at the asshole's door. The night's events bringing back a mixture of rage and embarrassment. I stomp off before I risk running into him again.

I step out onto the street weaving between the morning commuters heading to work, and tourists heading down to the waterfront. The air is cool and smells like the forest after a spring rain and mixed with the salt from the sound. The morning sun is now hiding behind gray clouds, and I'm feeling complete bliss. All my friends in New York thought I was crazy for moving to Seattle.

"All it does is rain there." I can still hear them in my head.

But I don't care, I love the rain, and I love this city. I have since I was nine when on one of the few family vacations my father took my brother Hunter and I on to visit to my Aunt Rita when my uncle Chad was stationed in Tacoma. My dad took us fishing down by the pier. We ate crab legs at the Crab Pot, and a seagull attacked my brother for his food. It was one of the happiest times I can remember after my mom died.

I loved living in New York, don't get me wrong, but without Jake it didn't feel like home anymore. The moment I stepped off the plane here in Seattle I was home. There's a small town feel about it here. The people are warm and welcoming, and it's just what I needed. New York is one of the best cities in the world, but it's hard and unforgiving and can eat you alive if you aren't careful. I needed to escape before it devoured me.

I round the corner, smiling, when I spot my favorite little

coffee shop, Lucy's. I quicken my pace, needing a massive dose of caffeine in the form of a vanilla latte. I open the door, and the strand of bells hanging above the entry way announces my arrival. Stepping inside, the scent of fresh coffee and blueberry scones fill my senses, making me hum in delight. The morning rush has past and there's just a couple people on laptops sitting by the windows. As I make my way to the counter, the bright eyed and perky owner, Lucy, pops up from the pastry case, greeting me with her warm welcoming smile.

"Good morning, sweetness. Your usual?" she asks.

"Yes please, and this time make it a triple," I reply, taking a seat at one of the empty tables.

I discovered Lucy's coffee shop one afternoon while out sightseeing in Pike's Place Market. I was walking down the rows of fresh fruit and vegetable stands, admiring the rainbow of colors, when I smelled the intoxicating scent of coffee and chocolate coming from her little shop. I ducked into her quaint little shop and it was warm and tranquil. The walls were covered with artwork and photographs from local artists, and along the back wall there were rows of shelves lined with books and funky little knick-knacks for sale. The bay of windows lining the front of the shop gave you the perfect view of the flower vendors that line the streets of the market. In the middle of the shop stood the coffee bar with pastry cases replete with handmade cupcakes, scones, cookies, and macaroons in every color of the rainbow. I instantly fell in love with the place.

"Rough night I take it?" She hands me my latte and plate with two blueberry scones then joins me at my table.

Over the past nine months, I've spent every morning at Lucy's drinking coffee while watching the tourists outside taking pictures and oohing and awing as they walked the streets. It also gave me the chance to get to know Lucy. Lucy is a petite, goofy brunette with these big brown eyes and a sweet smile that has all the men drooling over themselves.

She recognized me immediately on that first day, having read all my books. After her initial fangirl moment, and having me autograph her entire collection of my books, we started chatting and discovered we had quite a lot in common—both having lost the great loves of our lives. She lost her husband, Colton four years ago in Iraq, during what was supposed to be his final tour of duty. She moved back to Seattle wanting to raise her six-year-old daughter, Bailey, near her hometown where her family still lives. She's become a shoulder for me to lean on now that I'm away from my brother Hunter.

"You could say that. Remember the neighbor I was telling you about, Brian."

"Oh yeah, the man-whore."

"So we finally met last night." I can't even hide my disdain as the words come out of my mouth.

"Oh no, what happened?" She flashes me a concerned look.

I start rehashing the story of my run-in with Brian, starting with him answering the door in nothing but a sheet, the argument, him telling me I was jealous. As soon as I get to the part about me showing up at his door half naked, Lucy bursts into a full hardy laugh.

"Thanks for the support, friend. My nipples were out for the whole damn world to see and all you can do is laugh," I huff before taking a sip of my coffee.

"What? It's damn funny. And will make for a great story to tell your children about how you met their father." She chuckles, stealing a piece of my scone.

"Screw you and stop stealing my food." I pull my plate of scones away from her greedy hands. "What the hell makes you think I remotely like this asshole?"

"Well, because this is the most fired up I've seen you get since meeting you. Your mouth might be telling me you hate him, but considering how flushed you are just talking about this guy tells me otherwise. You like him," she teases.

"I do not. This is rage. N . . . not I need his d . . . dick in me." I stumble over my words, finding it hard to form a coherent sentence. I can feel my body growing hotter, making it more difficult to plead my case of just how much this guy irritates me. "He's an asshole, and I don't want him anywhere near me or my panties."

Liar. You big fat liar Brooke.

"I was just messing with you, but damn he really did get under your skin. And you so want him to rip you out of those pretty little panties of yours," she teases. "I like this flustered side of you. It's rather entertaining."

"Oh my God, can we please just change the subject? I can't go to my meeting with my publisher acting like an irate crazy person. I did enough of that last night."

"Oh shit, he finally got in touch with you. Have you been able to get anything down on paper?"

"Not a fucking word and I'm freaking out."

My muse came to me when I met Jake, and I'm starting to think she died right along with him.

Lucy slides her hand over mine and gives me a sincere smile. "I know you've been through a lot since losing Jake. I, for one, know what it's like to have to pick up the pieces of your life after losing the love of your life. In the short time I've gotten to know you, I can tell you're a badass lady who'll come out of this ten times stronger. You will find your muse again, I know you will. You got this, babe."

"Thank you, Lucy. I hope you're right." I return her smile, letting her words sink in. Lucy, my sweet, ball busting, optimistic new friend. She's definitely going to be good for my ego.

"I know I'm right. How about you come blow off some steam with Lucky and me tonight? Ryder will be there too."

She playfully wiggles her eyebrows at me. "I'm sure he'd be happy to help give you some inspiration for your writing."

I roll my eyes at her statement. Ryder is a sweet, gorgeous as hell cop with the Seattle PD that I met a few weeks ago in Lucy's shop. He has big blue puppy dog eyes, and from what I can tell in his uniform, he's built like a fucking God. But sadly, he did nothing in the downstairs department for me because, apparently, I only have a thing for assholes now.

"I don't know how much fun I will be."

"Come on Brooke, just one drink, please?" She bats her lashes and pouts her lips at me.

"How can I say no to that? Okay fine, one drink," I concede.

Lucy squeals in delight, throwing her arms around my neck squeezing me tight. Damn, she has a strong grip for such a tiny little thing. "I promise you'll have a great time."

⋆ ⋆ ⋆

My foot nervously taps against the marble floors of the waiting room at Barrett Publishing. My palms are sweating, and the knots in my stomach are twisting tighter with every second that passes.

The moment the door opens and Michael steps out from his office, my heart leaps into my throat and all I want to do is bolt, but it's too late, he's already spotted me.

"Miss McCoy, please come in." His monotone voice is making me even more nervous.

I nervously stand up from my chair and run my hands down along my dress, straightening out the wrinkles before starting my slow walk toward the office. Each step feels like my shoes are made out of cement.

I follow Michael into his office. The room is far warmer than I expected. There are floor to ceiling cherry wood bookshelves covering every inch of wall space. Dark green carpeting with a gold filigree diamond pattern leading the way to a massive mahogany desk sitting in front of a picture window that overlooks the city. It reminds me of the library my mom had in our old house and it's oddly relaxing.

"Miss McCoy, please take a seat," he orders pointing to the green and blue tweed chairs sitting in front of his desk.

I swallow back the lump in my throat as I take a seat. Crossing my legs at my ankles, my hands fidget in my lap.

"I'm glad I could finally get you into the office today."

"I apologize for the delay, Mr. Barrett. I've been so busy with moving . . ."

"I don't care to hear your excuses, Miss McCoy," he interjects. "Look, Brooke, we have given you ample time to grieve and get through the loss of your fiancé, but we can't keep extending your deadline on this new project any longer. We need to see some pages from you by the end of the month or we will have to release you from your contract."

The panic rips through me. I've lost so much over the past two years; I can't lose the one thing that keeps me sane. If I couldn't write books and share them with the world I would be completely lost.

"I promise I will have new pages to my editor very soon. I just need a little more time, please," I beg.

"All we have been giving you is time. You have sixty days to get us the new chapters."

"I will get them to you as soon as possible," I promise. *How the hell am I going to pull eight chapters out of my ass before the end of the month?*

CHAPTER FOUR

Brian

"YOU'RE RECKLESS AND A DANGER to this entire department," the Captain snarls, pointing an angry finger in my direction.

I sit back in my chair, arms folded in front of my chest, and a relaxed smirk on my face. I have this speech completely memorized. I've heard it at least once a week since I transferred to the second precinct four years ago. Oh wait, here comes my favorite part.

"There are rules and procedures, Gamble. If you can't follow them, I won't hesitate to fire your ass."

He's been saying that for years and I'm still fucking here. I'm the best damn cop the Seattle PD has. They will never fire me. I've wanted to be a cop since birth. My grandfather was a cop, all my aunts are cops, and my dad, before he was gunned down, was a cop. It's in my blood, it's what I was always meant to do and, God damn, I'm fucking good at it.

"Come on Cap, you and I both know if you were in my shoes and had seen what that animal did to his wife and daughter, you would've knocked him on his ass too."

To be honest, that piece of human waste deserved more than just getting knocked out after what he did to his wife and eight-year-old daughter. He's fucking lucky my partner pulled me off of him when he did or he'd be in a body bag right now. I've been a cop for six years, and I've seen some pretty fucked up shit, but when it comes to someone abusing women, and especially kids, that's where I draw the fucking line.

"Any officer in here would've wanted to do what you did if they'd come onto the scene that you and Callahan had. But they would've had the restraint not to knock the guy out while he was still in cuffs. Gamble, you're a great cop, one of our best. But you have to start using your head, because, one of these times I'm not going to be able to save your ass. For now, you're suspended for three days."

"Are you fucking kidding me, Cap? This is fucking bullshit," I hiss standing up from my chair and knocking it to the ground. The anger is surging through my body. How dare he tell me how to do my fucking job? I eat, sleep, and breathe law enforcement, so I bend the rules every once in a while. At least I get the job done, unlike this fucking paper pusher who hasn't seen action since he sold out to be a desk jockey.

"You brought this on yourself, Gamble. You're lucky it's just a suspension. Now go home and cool off," he barks back at me.

I flash him a nasty glare before turning to leave. Slamming the door behind me, I storm off to the locker room.

"This is fucking bullshit," I growl pulling open my locker. Grabbing my gym bag out and throwing it across the empty room, I watch as it slides to the feet of my partner, Ryder.

"I see your meeting with the Captain went well?" He chuckles, picking up my bag and setting it on the wooden bench in front of the lockers.

"I got fucking suspended for three days because I'm the only cop around this fucking precinct with the balls do what needs to be done!"

"I don't know why you're getting your panties in a bunch

about getting suspended. It's not exactly a new thing for you. You've been getting your ass handed to you since we were kids."

Ryder and I have been best friends since kindergarten, when I asked if he wanted to go lay under the monkey bars on the playground and look up the girls' dresses. That was the first day we got sent to the principal's office. From that day forward we were known as Double Trouble. Teachers would beg the principle to put us in separate classes. He has become like a brother to me, and there's no one I'd trust more to have my back than Ryder. But he can also be a giant pain in the ass.

"Fuck you, man," I growl.

"Hey, don't get pissed at me. You know I'm behind you on this."

"I'm sorry man."

"Don't worry about it. I know it's been a rough couple of days for you. First you get slapped by your neighbor, then you get suspended." His laugh echoes through the locker room.

"I told you not to bring that crazy bitch up again." I had made the mistake of telling Ryder about my run-in with my neighbor and he hasn't been able to drop it.

"What? It's fucking hilarious. Finally, a woman who didn't fall for the Gamble charm. If I ever meet this woman, I'm going to ask for her autograph."

I roll my eyes in annoyance. "If I were you, I'd stay as far away from her as possible. She's fucking crazy."

"Why are you getting so bent out of shape about this chick? I've literally seen a woman knee you in the balls and you just laughed it off." His eyes light up like a light bulb has just gone off in his head. "Oh, I get it now. She said no and that bugs you. No one has ever said no to the great Gamble. Which of course, pisses you off to no end, and I'm sure it only makes you want her more."

"Plenty of women have said no to me before, so your logic

is off base," I scoff.

"That might be true, but you like this one. Whether you want to admit it or not, she's gotten under your skin."

"Can we please just drop this? She's a bitch and I want nothing to do with her. So fucking drop it."

Liar. The truth is, he's right . . . but I would never tell him that.

She's gotten under my skin and her telling me 'no' has only made it worse. There's just something about her I can't shake.

"Fine, I'll drop it." He puts his hands up to surrender. "You coming out tonight?"

"Yeah, after the day I've had, I need to get fucking wasted."

* * *

The drive home only adds to my frustration. I'm stuck in traffic, the radio is just talk, and I have nothing to keep my mind occupied. Nothing to keep the voices in my head at bay. The nagging shrill voice of my ex telling me what a pathetic piece of garbage I am, along with the fact that I'm a worthless cop, and I destroy everything I touch is radiating through my brain. Fuckin' hate that bitch for getting in my head.

I sit through the light on Fourth and Pike for the third time, dreading what I know is to come but instead of the nagging voice, I get a flash of Brooke's sparkling blue eyes. Yes, the crazy bitch has a name. On my way to work, I stopped at the row of mailboxes that line a wall in the lobby and found her name. I don't know why I did it. I guess I wanted a name to go with the crazy eyes, or for the eventual restraining order.

But the thing is, she didn't seem crazy. Being a cop, I deal with an array of crazy on a daily basis. I can read people better than anyone and after one glance at Brooke I knew I wasn't the only reason for her outburst last night. The dark circles under her eyes telling me it had been longer than three days since she'd had a goodnight's sleep. And behind the daggers in her eyes, I could see sadness. For some reason, I had this overwhelming urge to be the one to make it go away. But after our fight I'm sure she hates me even more. God, why did I have to open my big mouth and tell her she was basically a pent up nun? More importantly, why the fuck did I care that I pissed her off?

I've pissed off my fair share of women and have been slapped and kneed in the balls more times than I can remember. I always manage to shake it off, but knowing that Brooke hates me makes me sick to my stomach.

I finally pull into my building. As I walk out of the elevator, I can't help but walk by her door. I pause in front of it for a moment, wanting to knock and try an apology for what I said to her last night. But the sting of her slap rings along my cheek again so I move past her door. She's just like all the rest of them.

"Don't get wrapped up in your emotions Gamble, she's not worth it," I say to myself as I open my door.

As soon as I step inside I hear the jingle of Lola's collar as she comes bounding out of my bedroom. Lola is my gray and white Pit Bull puppy. I got her three months ago, after Ryder and I busted a dog fighting ring in the outskirts of Seattle. While we were helping animal rescue with the dogs, I saw Lola shaking and whimpering in one of the cages. She was too afraid to come to anyone else, but when she saw me, she came and sat at my feet and wouldn't leave until I picked her up. It was love at first sight, and she's the only woman I trust with my heart.

I kneel down, rubbing behind her ears while she licks my face, her tail wagging in excitement to see me. "How's my favorite girl today?"

She barks then licks my face again before trotting over to her food dish, pushing it in my direction, letting me know she's ready to eat. I walk into the kitchen and pour a cup of kibble into her bowl then head back to my bedroom and lay on my bed, letting out a frustrated sigh. My quiet room is disturbed when my phone rings. I pull my phone out of my pocket and see my mom's number on the screen.

"Hey Mom, how's it going?" I answer trying to hide the frustration in my voice.

"Hello, my sweet boy. I'm doing just fine. But you, on the other hand, don't sound so good."

"How do you always know when I'm hiding things from you?"

"Because I'm your mother and mothers always know when their children are in distress. Now tell me what's going on?"

"I got suspended today."

"Oh Brian, not again." I can hear the disappointment in her voice. "What happened this time?"

I rest my hand over my eyes, rubbing my temples with my thumb and forefinger as I tell her about the scene Ryder and I walked into. The father hovering over his eight-year-old daughter's limp body. Her face bruised and bloody, and the mom equally beaten screaming at him to stop. He was high on meth and just as drunk. He wouldn't stop screaming that he was going to kill them both, and even tried lunging for the mom after I'd cuffed him. That's when I snapped and knocked him out. I hated going on these calls, no one wants to see an innocent child half-beaten to death by the one person who's supposed to be protecting them. These scenes always gave me nightmares for days afterward.

"Oh sweetheart, that's horrible. Are the little girl and her mom going to be all right?" Her disappointment fades into concern.

"I called the hospital, they're both in intensive care. The mom has a severe concussion, a broken cheekbone, and a broken arm. The daughter has a broken nose, three cracked ribs, and a concussion. But they'll both be okay. The women's center is going to take them in once they're released from the hospital. How can anyone do that to a child? I just wanted to kill the guy, he's supposed to be protecting her." I can feel my anger starting to surge through me again.

"I know it's an awful situation. But you got that sweet girl and her mom away from that monster, and they're going to have a new start to a better life, thanks to you and Ryder. Don't focus on the negative or the suspension. You did the right thing, even if your captain can't see it. I know for a fact your father would be so proud of what you did," she says trying to reassure me.

"Do you think so?"

My father was gunned down during a drug bust when I was six. So I never really got to know what kind of a man or cop he was outside of the stories my mom and his cop buddies would tell me. But from what I gathered, he was known to bend the rules too.

"I know he would be. You're a great cop, Brian. Don't ever let anyone ever convince you otherwise. I love you, sweetheart."

"I love you too, Mom."

"Feel better son, and I'll talk to you soon."

I hang up with Mom and toss my phone on the bed, feeling a little bit better after our talk. She's right, because of me, that mom and her daughter are going to get the help they need, and that monster will never be able to terrorize them again.

I sit up, spotting Lola walking through the door, but instead of hopping up on the bed with me, she sits down in front of the wall behind my bed. I cock an eyebrow up finding it odd. She starts scratching her paw along the stucco wall and begins whimpering. I get up from the bed and walk over to her.

"What are you doing, Lola?" And that's when I hear it, a soft moan coming from behind the wall. Moans that sound like sex moans. Maybe I was wrong about Brooke? Maybe she isn't a pent up nun.

"Oh fuck, Brian," she screams.

My eyes widen and I press my greedy ear to the wall and look down at Lola, who's staring up at me with a curious look in her eye. I listen carefully, trying to hear if there's someone else in the room with her, but all I can hear are her moans and the chanting of my name, demanding me to fuck her harder. I can't believe it; the crazy bitch is having a sex dream about me. But what's even harder to believe is that I'm imagining what I was doing to her—my dick growing painfully hard at the image of her on all fours, ass in the air and begging for my cock.

Get it the fuck together Brian. No matter how much you want to fuck her right now, she's still the enemy. I think I need another cold shower.

* * *

Showered and still frustrated, I step out of my apartment just in time to spot a leggy brunette walking toward the elevator. I'm instantly drawn to her like a magnet. My eyes trail up her long, lean legs, and I'm already imagining what they'll feel like wrapped around my waist. Her soft curves are covered in a light pink dress, hitting just above her knees. Such a lovely dress, it's a shame it'll be lying in pieces on my bedroom floor later. I follow behind her, watching the confident sway of her hips. It's almost hypnotic.

The elevator doors open just as we arrive; she steps inside first. She turns and seeing her face is like a punch to the gut. "Crazy bitch," I whisper under my breath. She looks different fully clothed. No wonder I didn't recognize her. As soon as she notices me, her soft expression turns hard, and her eyes are like daggers, staring me down as I step into the elevator. She hits the button for the lobby and moves closer to the wall and away from me. I stay on my side of the elevator, fighting with myself to not say anything. But I've never been one to hold my tongue.

"I think you owe me an apology." I say breaking the silence.

She turns to look at me, her face is red hot with anger. She kinda looks cute when she's mad.

"In what delusional world makes you think I owe you an apology?" she snarls.

"I believe it was you that slapped me in the face," I snap back.

"Look here asshole, you're lucky it was just a slap to the face after what you said to me. I'm not some pent up jealous bitch."

"If the shoe fits, sweetheart. I call it as I see it." I flash her a confident smirk.

"Oh, you want to play that game. Okay, I'll play along. You wanna know what I see when I look at you?"

"Bring it on sweetheart, I'd love to hear this." Folding my arms in front of me, I take a few steps closer, invading her space.

"I see a sad pathetic man who's had his heart broken by some nasty bitch, but instead of dealing with the emotional wreckage she's left in her wake, he goes out and bangs anything with tits then drops them on their asses as payback for his broken heart. It's fucking pathetic."

"If you were a man right now . . ." I growl trailing off, stepping closer and forcing her up against the wall of the elevator. My rage surging through my body.

How dare she call me pathetic?

"What, you wanna hit me?" She gets up right in my face. The fire now igniting between us. "I dare you!" Her lips now inches from mine and, even as pissed off as I am at her right now, I can't fight my urge to taste those lips.

"Why are you such a bitch?" I whisper, licking my lips in anticipation.

"Why do you have to be such an asshole?" she retorts.

With that, my lips crash down onto hers as I pull her into my arms. Her body tenses at first, but as soon as our tongues meet in her warm mouth, her body relaxes, and her hands find their way into my hair, pulling me tighter against her mouth. Her lips are soft and sweet, her tongue warm and velvety against mine. She tastes so damn good; a man could get addicted.

I know I should push away, but I can't get enough of how good she tastes and how much I want to have her right here and now. Finally, be the one to make her moan and scream not just the dream of me. I press her against the wall, hands slipping under her dress and grabbing two handfuls of her gorgeous ass. Holding her tight against me so she could feel the effect she's having on me. I'm fucking rock hard. Before we can go any further, the elevator chimes, signaling our arrival at the main lobby. She pushes me away, looking slightly disoriented and breathing hard.

"This never happened," she murmurs, then quickly runs out of the elevator.

"Whatever you say, sweetheart," I call after her, watching as she runs out the glass doors. And as much as I hate to admit it, this crazy bitch is starting to grow on me.

CHAPTER FIVE

Brooke

"THIS DAY JUST KEEPS GETTING better and better," I whisper to myself, banging my head against the wooden bar. The kiss Brian and I shared in the elevator is still lingering on my lips. I can't believe he kissed me and, more importantly, I can't believe I kissed him back. I want to hate him for it, but God, his kiss felt so fucking good. I haven't been kissed like that in, well . . . ever.

Jake was a great kisser but nothing like the way Brian kissed me. It was so intense and full of need . . . like he needed me to fucking breathe. Lord help me, I can still feel my desire for more of him soaking through my panties. I've never met a man that both frustrates me and turns me on the way Brian does.

The perky-for-a-bartender brings me my drink and flashes me a pitiful smile. I don't need your pity, bitch, just keep bringing me booze. I grab the glass of whiskey and, as I'm taking my first sip, I hear a familiar voice coming from behind me.

"Wow Brooke, that beer is looking a little flat." Lucky teases, sliding up to the bar next to me with Lucy not far behind.

"It's not beer, it's whiskey." I put the glass to my lips and take another long slow sip. The amber liquor burning my throat all the way down.

"Jesus, you're hardcore, Brooke," she says with a laugh.

I met Lucky through Lucy a few weeks ago. The two of them grew up together on Bainbridge Island, they were practically sisters. and they sure fought like sisters too. It was pretty entertaining watching them bicker with each other. Lucky is the beautiful blonde model type, with hazel eyes and the most beautiful rose and lace tattoos on her arms. She's also wildly inappropriate and has no filter when it comes to giving you her opinion, which is what I love most about her. What I also find interesting about Lucky is that by day, she teaches painting and pottery at a small art school in West Seattle and, on the weekends, she strips at Blue Moon, a high-end strip club. I still have yet to get the full story as to why she likes stripping. But I'm sure since it's Lucky that it'll be entertaining.

"Leave her alone, Lucky. She had a rough day," Lucy chimes. "I guess your meeting with your publisher didn't go well?"

"No, it didn't go well." I take another swig of my drink. "But that is not why I am drinking. This is because I had another run in with my asshole neighbor in the elevator on my way down here."

"Oh fuck! What happened this time?" Lucy's eyes widen and her mouth drops open in shock.

"Wait! What neighbor?" Lucky asks curiously.

Before I can say a word, Lucy begins filling Lucky in on my embarrassing encounter with Brian. If she thought that was hilarious, she's really going to love what just went down in the elevator. I'm not even going to mention the crazy hot sex dream I had about Brian during my nap.

"The asshole had the balls to ask if she wanted to join them."

Lucky looks back at me, giggling to herself. "So did you?" she asks.

"Lucky!" Lucy shouts, reaching behind me to slap her on

the shoulder.

"What? It's an honest question," she says rubbing her arm.

"No. I did not bang my neighbor and his skank. I know I haven't had sex in two years, but I'm not about to hop into bed with my asshole neighbor." I down the last of my whiskey and can already feel the warmth of my buzz taking over. I look up from my glass, seeing a puzzled look on Lucky's face.

"Wait . . . What?" Her hazel eyes dart around as she tries to process my statement. "Brooke, are you telling me you haven't had sex in two years . . . two years?"

I nod yes, waving the bartender down for a refill of whiskey.

"So what you are saying is no dick has entered any part of your body for twenty-four months."

"Yep."

"I think I need to sit down." She slumps down onto her barstool and asks the bartender to bring her a shot of tequila then looks back at me, her eyes widened in disbelief. "How is that even possible? You're a gorgeous piece of ass. So I'm sure men have been throwing themselves at you to get a chance with you." She downs her shot then signals for another. "I mean, shit, even I would take you into the bathroom of this bar and go to town on you . . . two years!"

"Don't listen to her, Brooke. Lucky can barely go twenty-four hours without getting plowed. Not everyone jumps back into dating or having sex right away after losing someone they love."

As comforting as Lucy's words were, even I know two years is a hell of a long time to go without sex with an actual man. My vibrator gets the job done, but sometimes you just need to feel the touch of a man. Someone to hold you and kiss you while they make love to you.

"No, don't listen to her. Lucy barely made it ten months after Colton died before she went on a manhunt. But seriously, two years . . . God, you're practically a virgin again." Lucky reaches down to the hem of my dress and starts to lift up the pink fabric. "Does it even still work?"

I slap her hand away. "Yes, of course, it still works."

"How do you know if you haven't let her out to play?" She gives me a sideways glance before downing her second shot.

"Because my panties are still wet from the asshole kissing me in the elevator." I cringe when I realize what just slip from my lips.

"Oh my God, he kissed you? Like on the lips, kissed you?" Lucy shrieks over the music, and I hide behind my hands from the few people that look our direction.

"Yes. We were in the elevator arguing because he said I owed him an apology, and the next thing I knew we're in each other's faces. The electricity was sparking between us and, before I know it, he was kissing me." I let out a quiet sigh. "I wanted to push him away, but God, it felt so damn good. It made me feel wanted, that is something I haven't felt in such a long time."

I bang my head against the bar. "I'm so confused. My head is telling me to hate him, but my body is telling me to fuck him into next Tuesday. He's the first man since Jake that's had this big of an effect on me. Maybe being away from the game for so long has my body all confused. Why couldn't it react this way with Ryder, he's actually nice to me."

"Did I just hear someone say my name?"

Springing up in my seat, I spin around, meeting the sparkling blue-eyed gaze of Ryder. His lips are curled up in a sly smirk. I feel my face flush, hoping he didn't hear all of what I'd said. I eye him up and down for a moment, I've never seen him out of uniform before. He looks completely different. He's dressed in dark jeans and a tight gray shirt that hugs his muscular frame in all the right places and shows off the sleeve of tattoos he has along his right arm. His dark sandy locks that are usually combed back are now spiked up, looking like he's just had a good fucking before heading to the bar. His chiseled jawline has a whisper of stubble. He's sexy as hell, but still, even seeing him like this is doing nothing for me. Nothing like what Brian had done to me in that elevator.

"Brooke was just telling us about how she wants to bang her new neighbor," Lucky teases.

Ryder laughs, shaking his head at Lucky's statement knowing she's full of crap. But I still slump down in my chair ready to die of embarrassment.

"Lucky, leave the poor girl alone. And you and I both know she's saving herself for me. That's if I can get her to say yes to dinner first." He flashes me a wink then waves the bartender down to order a beer.

Ryder has been trying to persuade me into going out on at least one date with him. But in the little time I've gotten to know Ryder, I keep getting a sense that he's just using me to show Lucky what she's missing out on. I can see he's crazy about her from the way he looks at her and how he hangs off every word she says. He wants more with her, but Lucky doesn't strike me as the relationship type.

Lucy detects my discomfort and diverts the conversation off me and onto Lucky, asking about one of her creepy clients from the strip club. I relax back in my chair and sip on my drink listening to their conversation and the music coming from the dance floor. I'm so distracted I don't even notice the tall figure that has worked his way between me and Ryder. It isn't until I hear Lucy's loud laughter that I look over and see him. My heart leaps into my throat when I realize who's standing just inches away from me. I recognize the short mussed dark brown hair, the brown eyes that could light up the night sky. and the cocky grin that I just want to slap off his face. "Brian," I whisper under my breath.

Just then he turns and looks down at me, a condescending smirk slides across his lips. "Well this must be my lucky day. Hey Ace."

"What are you doing here?" I growl, staring him down.

Ryder turns his attention from Lucky and smiles when he spots Brian. "Hey man, I see you found us. Oh, hey, you haven't met Brooke yet. Brooke this my partner and best friend Brian. Brian this—"

"Oh, Brooke and I are old friends." He smiles, with an amused look in his eyes.

"Wait! How do you two know each other?" Ryder asks.

I'm completely frozen, my mouth gaping open. I watch as Lucky and Lucy say hello to Brian. My mind is racing. How do they know him? How did they not know it was him I was telling them about? What the hell is going on?

"Brooke's that neighbor I was telling you about."

Ryder's head snaps back to look at me. "You're Crazy Bitch?"

"What did you just call me?" I snarl, feeling my rage kicking in again.

Before I can snap into full bitch mode, Ryder is pulling me into his arms, giving me a huge bear hug. "I've been dying to meet the woman that finally put this asshole in his place. You are my hero." He squeezes me tighter, lifting me off my feet, and I can hear Lucy and Lucky putting together the pieces of what's going on. My rage now turning to embarrassment, wondering what he's told them about me.

I pull away from Ryder's grasp, trying to fight back the tears that are now welling in my eyes. I can't believe he told people I was a crazy bitch. No one has ever been so callous to me. I just wanted him to keep the fucking noise down. He's the one that kept pushing my buttons.

"I can't deal with this. I'm getting out of here." I can't hold onto my tears for much longer, and I don't want to give him the satisfaction of seeing me cry. I grab my bag and fight my way through the crowd, ignoring Lucy and Lucky calling for me to come back. I burst through the back door out into the alley behind the bar. I lean back against the brick wall of the bar, breathing in the cool night air trying to calm myself before walking home. This whole situation is getting completely out of control, and I don't know what to do to stop it. Other than move into a cave in the middle of the forest where no one would know me as The Crazy Bitch.

The back door of the bar opens again, and I think it's Lucy coming to find me, but when I look up, it's Brian standing before me. Why can't he just leave me alone?

"If you're here to make fun of me some more, you can turn around and go back inside because I don't have the energy to fight with you anymore," I say wiping the tears away from my cheeks.

"I'm not here to fight with you. I'm here to apologize."

Apologize? He wants to apologize to me? This feels like a trick, but my mind is intrigued. "I'm listening."

"Look, Brooke, I'm sorry for being such an asshole to you before. I was completely out of line. You were frustrated and exhausted, and I only made things worse, so I'm sorry. Do you think we could start over?"

I can see the sincerity in his eyes and I know he's truly sorry. Maybe he isn't as bad as I thought he was.

"I think we could do that. I'm sorry for slapping you and calling you out in the elevator," I say giving him a warm smile.

"I kind of deserved it, and you were spot on in your judgment of me." He chuckles softly. "Hi. I'm Brian Gamble." He holds his right hand out to me.

"It's nice to meet you, Brian. I'm Brooke McCoy." I slide my hand into his and a familiar pulse of electricity courses through my body, just like it had in the elevator when I felt his hands slip under my dress.

"So, friends?" he asks.

"Have you ever been friends with someone you've made out with in an elevator?"

His laugh echoes through the quiet alley. "No, but there's a first time for everything. I'm willing to give it a try if you are?" He flashes me another crooked smile.

Damn, that smile is sexy as hell. Calm yourself Brooke.

"I'm willing to try." I return his smile, feeling myself starting to relax again.

"Great! So how about we kiss and make up?" He smirks, wiggling his eyebrows at me.

I can't help but laugh and shake my head at his question. "Friends don't kiss."

"I know; I was just teasing you. But I did get you to laugh."

"That you did, and I kinda needed that." I giggle again. Funny and sexy, that's a dangerous combination.

"Do you want to come back inside, and I'll buy you a drink?"

"That's sweet, but I think I'm going to head home. It's been a long day, and I should try and get some sleep." As much as I want to go back inside with him, I just need some space to process finding out my asshole neighbor isn't the asshole I'd pegged him to be, and that he's also best friends with my new friends. This fucking day is throwing me for a loop.

"Do you want me to walk you home?"

"No, that's okay. You should go back inside and enjoy the rest of your night."

"All right. Sweet dreams." He flashes me a wink.

"Um . . . thanks." I turn and start to walk away, a little confused by his last statement.

"Oh, and Brooke? I hope I'm good tonight," he calls out.

I stop dead in my tracks. Oh, fuck! He heard me through the wall. Now I really need to go crawl under a rock.

CHAPTER SIX

Brian

IT WAS AFTER MIDNIGHT WHEN I finally made it home. The house was dark and quiet, and it made me miss the days when Jillian would wait up for me. I tossed my keys on the counter and grabbed a beer out of the fridge. Taking a sip, I walked back to the bedroom, pausing when I saw a soft glow coming from under the door. At first I thought maybe Jilly did wait up and had a surprise waiting for me. But as I got closer that was when I heard the soft moans. I quietly stepped closer to the door and I could hear the moans growing louder and more ragged. I carefully turned the knob on the door and opened it just a crack and, I saw her, bent over our bed. Her bright red hair falling over her face. Her screams of ecstasy making my stomach turn as I watched her getting fucked to within an inch of her life by our Captain. She looked up and saw me watching from the crack in the door. An amused smile was painted across her face. "Loser," she mouthed.

And that's when I spring up from my bed, covered in sweat, and breathing hard. My eyes begin to focus and I realize I'm back in my bedroom in my apartment, and it was just a dream. It's been five years since the night I walked in on my ex, fucking my former Captain in the bed we once shared, and it still haunts me. Lola hops up on my bed. She must have sensed my distress because she curls up in my lap then licks my face in an attempt to make me feel better.

I met Jillian in the police academy. Back then she was a different person, she was confident and caring and didn't take shit from anyone. And feisty as all hell, which was one of the things that drew me to her. She was the first woman I ever really loved, and I was almost going to ask her to marry me. But after we graduated from the academy she started to change. Her competitive side began to show more and more with the other officers on the force. And once I started passing her up, getting promoted before her, she started to resent me for it. She started taking her frustrations and confidence issues out on me and anyone else who got in her way. At first I just brushed it off as stress of the job, but once she started making me question who I was and if being a cop was really what I was meant to do, I started wondering if being with her was really worth it. I got my answer that night. I wasn't her boyfriend anymore, I was just a road block to her and she didn't care how much she hurt me if it meant she got what she wanted. I walked out of the house we shared that night and never looked back, but she still manages to get in my head.

I glance over at my alarm, it's seven in the morning, and there's no way after that nightmare I'll be able to go back to sleep, so I decide to go for a run to help clear my head.

As I slip on my running shorts, I hear a soft knock on my front door. I head out to the living room, wondering who could possibly be at my door this damn early. Opening the door, I feel the nagging voice in my head fade away when I see a smiling Brooke standing at my doorstep. I notice her deep blue eyes immediately. They're sparkling with intensity and look happier than the last time I saw her at my door. My eyes move down to her beautiful full lips and I'm instantly taken back to our kiss in the elevator. Less than twenty-four hours ago, those warm sweet lips were devouring my mouth. With that image, my dick begins to stir. Down boy, remember she's just a friend.

"Hey, Brooke. To what do I owe this lovely surprise?"

She softly smiles holding up a plate of what looks to be donuts. "I just thought I'd bring over a little peace offering." She looks me up and down and pulls her bottom lip between her teeth as her eyes linger on my bare chest before meeting my gaze again. "Oh, I'm sorry, did I wake you?"

"No, I was just getting up. So what did you bring me?"

"I made a batch of bacon maple donuts."

My eyes widen and my stomach growls in anticipation. "You had me at bacon. Get your sexy ass in here," I say stepping aside to let her in.

Closing the door, I follow her to the kitchen, and she has that sexy confident sway in her walk again, and it has me in a trance already. She's dressed in a pair of denim cut-off shorts, a casual pink T-shirt, and a pair of white chucks. I love girls who wear chucks. Her long dark hair is pulled up in a messy bun on top of her head, and she has a handprint of flour smeared across her ass. Damn, is there anything this woman doesn't look sexy in?

"How about I make us some coffee?" I suggest. Needing any excuse to keep from ripping her out of her clothes and fucking her on my kitchen island.

"That would be fantastic."

"So did you make these yourself?" I ask eyeing the plate of donuts as she sets it down on the bar. I'm trying not to drool over how good they look and how much I'd love to lick the icing off her gorgeous body.

"I did. I couldn't sleep last night and when I can't sleep, I bake."

"Sounds like I'm not the only one with sleeping issues." I flip on the coffee pot and feel her eyes on me, and it feels oddly calming.

"So why couldn't you sleep? Late night with one of your girls?" she asks and I can hear a hint of jealousy in her tone.

"No. Just happens from time to time. Besides, the only girl in my bed these days is my dog, Lola." I point over at Lola as she walks out of my bedroom. I hold my breath hoping she won't attack Brooke like she does all the other women I've brought home. She's a jealous little thing. But she doesn't go after Brooke, instead, sits at Brooke's feet and begs for her to pick her up.

"Oh my God, she's so cute." Brooke's face lights up as she bends down to pick up Lola. As soon as Lola's in her arms, she proceeds to excitedly lick Brooke's face. "You are quite the little love bug. I bet you get lots of girls for your daddy."

"Actually, she doesn't normally like a lot of people. This is the first time I've seen her let anyone but me pick her up." I usually I have to lock her in her crate when people are over. I've lost count of how many times she's bitten Ryder when he comes over.

"I don't believe that for a second, she's just so sweet. How old is she?"

"Nine months. I found her while doing a raid on a dog fighting ring. I was the only one she'd come to when animal rescue was loading up the dogs to take them back to the shelter. Something told me she belonged with me, so I adopted her right then and there."

"How very noble of you," she says flashing me that beautiful smile of hers.

Brooke sets Lola down on the floor and looks around my apartment while I pour us a couple cups of coffee. I sip my mine, watching as she inspects the art on the walls.

"Let me guess, you were expecting whips, chains, and a sex swing?"

She throws her head back and laughs, and it's the most beautiful intoxicating sound I've ever heard. "More like pyramids of empty beer cans and posters of half-naked women bent over sports cars. Whips and chains are more my thing," she says matter-of-factly, and I can't tell if she's kidding. God, I hope she's not kidding.

She hops up on one of the bar stools and takes a sip of her coffee.

I grab one of the donuts and take a big bite. My eyes roll back in my head as I chew. The maple and bacon taking over all my senses. This is hands down the best thing I've ever eaten. "Oh my God, Brooke, this is the best damn thing I've ever had in my mouth." I take another big bite.

"Well, that's because you've never had me in your mouth," she says nonchalantly, taking a bite of her donut.

I take a sharp breath, choking on a piece of bacon. Did she really just say that? She looks over at me with a glint of concern in her eyes.

"Are you okay?"

I finally clear the chunk of bacon out of my windpipe. "Do you always say shit like that, or is it just me that brings that out in you?" I choke out.

"I'm sorry. I don't really have a filter on this thing." She points to her mouth. "I tend to just say what's on my mind without thinking about it sometimes."

"Oh, so what you're saying is that you really want to be in my mouth?" I cock a curious eyebrow up at her.

"No, I didn't say that. It's just—" Her face turns a bright shade of red.

"But you did say you speak what's on your mind, and clearly what's on your mind is to ride my face," I tease.

"I do not. Can we please just change the subject?" she says

hiding behind her coffee cup. She's fucking adorable when she's flustered. This friendship is going to be fun.

"Okay, okay. We can talk about how much you want to have sex with me later," I say flashing her a wink.

"Oh my God, stop! I don't want to have sex with you."

"That's not what I heard through my wall yesterday." I lean over the counter, getting nice and close to her face. "Did you dream about me last night? Is that why you couldn't sleep?" I whisper, watching her body shiver and her face flush even brighter. "Oh, you did. Such a naughty girl."

"I'm leaving." She stumbles getting up from her stool and starts to walk toward the door.

"Wait, Brooke, don't go." I run past her, stepping between her and the door. "I'm sorry. I took the teasing too far. Just the whole, you in my mouth thing, made me go into my usual Gamble mode. Please stay."

"No, I'm sorry. I don't know what it is when I'm around you. I either want to hit you or sleep with you." She looks up at me with those big doe eyes, and I quickly realize she's feeling the same way I am about this whole situation. Two days ago I hated her, but now I can't fight this feeling of wanting to fuck her.

"You know this friendship is doomed to go up in flames?"

"Probably, but just think how fun the ride will be."

Brooke grins and softly giggles. I got her to laugh again so that's a good sign.

"I really should be going. I'll see you around?"

"You know where to find me." I step out the way and open the door for her. She stops in front of me and turns to place a sweet kiss on my cheek. "I thought friends didn't kiss?"

"They can kiss on the cheek. Thanks for the coffee and the laugh."

She turns and walks away. I rub my hand along my cheek where she kissed me and it feels like her lips are permanently seared into my skin, and I want that feeling over every inch of me.

CHAPTER SEVEN

Brooke

AS SOON AS I HEAR Brian's door close behind me I bolt for the stairwell, needing to see my girls. What the hell just happened? One minute I'm bringing Brian a simple plate of donuts as a peace offering, and the next thing I know I'm blurting out that he's never had anything as good as me in his mouth. What is the matter with me? Every time I'm around Brian I lose all function of my brain and turn into a crazy horn dog.

I burst out of the door onto the busy street. My head's still spinning as I make my way down three blocks through the crowd to Lucy's. Opening the door, I almost run into a guy coming out. After quickly apologizing, he flashes me an evil glare. I step inside scanning the small coffee shop for Lucy, who isn't at her usual station behind the coffee counter. Thankfully, the place is empty after the morning rush. As I walk around the coffee bar, Lucy comes walking out of the back kitchen carrying a big tray of freshly baked cupcakes.

"Oh, hey darlin'. What happened last night?" she asks setting the tray down on the counter. "Gamble said you went home after your talk in the alley. I can't believe he was your asshole neighbor. Although, I should've known because it sounds like him."

I slump down into one of the bar stools across from Lucy. "Brian and I just talked. He apologized for being a jerk, and I apologized for being a bitch and slapping his face. We agreed to try to be friends."

"Wow! I'm impressed. You actually got Brian to say the words 'I'm sorry' and he wants to be friends? He hasn't wanted to be friends with a woman, well since he met Lucky and me when we were all five. He must really like you." She smiles while refilling the pastry display case with red velvet cupcakes.

"More like he just wants to fuck me."

"Would that be such a bad thing?" she asks peeking her head out from over the glass case.

I scowl at her. "Lucy, I don't want to be just another notch on his bedpost." I let out a frustrated sigh, grabbing one of the cupcakes. I peel back the wrapper and shove half the cake into my mouth.

"Look, Brooke, I've known Gamble since we were kids. He's like a brother to me, so I know firsthand that, yes, he may want to fuck you and, yes, he has banged his fair share of skanks over the past five years. But he has never apologized to anyone, even if he knows he's wrong. And him wanting to be friends with you is a huge deal, that means he likes you. Like really likes you and wants to get to know you."

"Do you really think so?" I ask.

"I know so. He wants to put in the effort to show you that he's not such a bad guy. He hasn't wanted to do that since the evil bitch broke his heart. Deep down, Brian is a good guy, and it showed last night. After you had stormed out of the bar, he looked genuinely concerned that he'd upset you. And after you left, you were all he could talk about."

"He did?"

"Yes. Look, Brooke, I'm not saying you have to jump into bed with him tomorrow, but maybe get to know him. Give him a chance to show you that he's not the asshole you think he is. You both aren't looking for anything serious right now, so what's the harm in having a little fun?"

Maybe she's right. But am I really ready for just having fun with a guy? Before meeting Brian, I hadn't even thought about dating or sex. Maybe all of this craziness with Brian is a sign that it's time I got back into the game.

"I guess I could give it a try, as long as I can stop myself from telling him he should put me in his mouth."

Her eyes widen and her mouth drops open. "You told him to what?"

"I went over there to bring him some donuts as a little peace offering. We were talking and it was going well. Then he says my donuts were the best thing he's had in his mouth and, before I could stop myself, I blurted out how it was because he'd never had me in his mouth."

Lucy bursts into laughter. "Oh God, I bet he got a kick out of that. Put me in your mouth," she squeals.

"I don't know what it is about this man that makes me lose all logical function of my brain. He smiles at me with those big brown eyes and those dimples . . . those fucking dimples, and I turn into a horny wreck. He's turning me into a hot fucking mess, and of course, he's getting a kick out of it, especially now that he's heard me having sex dreams about him."

"You're having sex dreams about him too?" She slams her hand down on the counter exuberantly. "Yep, you two are so going to bang then get married and have so many babies."

"God, I hate you," I groan shoving the rest of my cupcake into my mouth.

CHAPTER EIGHT

Brooke

I POUR MYSELF A GLASS of wine then walk back into my living room. I stare at the pile of wood panels and screws that are to be my new bookshelves. That is, if I can make it through the novel that's the building instructions from Ikea. The logical part of my brain is telling me I should run next door and ask Brian for help, but I may have been avoiding him for the past week. It's not like I don't want to be friends with him. It's just that, since meeting Brian, he has managed to start chipping away at the wall I had built after Jake passed. He has exposed emotions I haven't had to deal with in years and it's both painful and freeing at the same time. I'm still trying to wrap my brain around all of it, and I thought a little time away from Brian would help, but I keep wanting to see him. I'm utterly confused. I chug back my wine then set to work.

Just as I'm about to hammer in one of the pegs, I slam the hammer down hard onto my thumb, and the profanities begin to spew from my mouth and echo through my apartment. I bring my thumb to my mouth sucking on it—like that's really going to take the pain away—when I hear a knock on my door. I pull myself up from the floor, thumb still firmly planted in my mouth, as I walk over to the door. I check the peephole and my head jerks back when I spot Brian standing there. Damn, he must have heard me through the wall. So I can't really pretend I'm not home.

I open the door, meeting his brown-eyed gaze. His lips curling into a panty killer of a smile. He's dressed in cargo shorts, a gray Guns and Roses Concert T-shirt, and his dark brown hair is hidden under a backward baseball cap. God, he is so damn sexy.

"Hi Brian," I say returning his smile.

"Hey, Brooke. Are you okay? I thought I heard you scream," he replies with a hint of concern in his voice.

"I'm fine, I was just trying to put together my new bookshelves, and I hit my thumb with the hammer." I lift my hand up showing him injured thumb.

He grabs my hand. His touch radiates through my entire body. Bringing my hand up closer to his face, he inspects my thumb. "Doesn't look broken." His gaze softens as he kisses my thumb before releasing my hand. Yep, he's officially trying to kill me.

"Do you want some help?"

"No, it's fine. I can do it."

"Are you sure? I don't mind." There's that damn sexy smile again making the heat pool between my thighs. My head is telling me to send him on his way, but little Brooke is screaming at me to let him in.

Enough of this shit. Sorry brain you lose; I'm letting him in.

"Well, maybe some help would be good."

A relieved look washes over Brian's face as I step aside. I can't help but take a little peek at his cute little tight butt as he walks by. Giving me the urge to wanna bite it.

Brian steps further into the living room and his eyes widen when he sees the mess on the floor.

"Some help? It looks like Home Depot exploded in here. We are going to need a construction crew and a miracle." He laughs.

"I know, it's a disaster, and I'll totally understand if you want to run," I reply feeling slightly embarrassed.

Note to self—Don't drink and build furniture.

"I can make it up to you with beer and I'll even make you dinner."

"Sold! Now where's the screwdriver?"

* * *

Brian is putting the last of the screws into the third and final book shelf, while I'm in the kitchen distracting myself from the gorgeous piece of man flesh in my living room with a pot of meatballs. It's not really helping, I find myself looking at his arms. The way his muscles flex with every turn of the screwdriver makes me wish they were pinning me down on this counter while he screws me into submission. And don't even get me started on those nimble fingers of his, pushing inside me and working me to the fucking brink until I'm screaming his name.

I feel my body getting over heated at the image of Brian fucking my brains out. I can't actually leave to take a cold shower, so I walk over to the freezer and open the door, letting the cold air wash over me. Taking long deep breaths trying to calm myself.

"Brooke."

Brian's voice jolts me back to reality causing me to slam the freezer door shut. I run my hands through my hair and take one last calming breath before walking back over to the kitchen bar. "Do you need something?" I ask hoping he doesn't see how flushed I am.

"No. I was just asking you what brought you to Seattle."

"Oh sorry, I didn't hear you. I was getting some ice from the freezer." More like I was trying to crawl into the tiny space to keep from jumping your bones. "Well, it's kind of a weird story. You'll probably think I'm even crazier after hearing it."

"It can't be that weird," he replies hiding a soft chuckle.

"We'll see about that. It was about nine months ago when I got the idea to move. My friends back in New York thought it was time for me to start dating again and, at the time, I thought I was ready, so I agreed to go out on a blind date. The date was a complete disaster. The guy was a total narcissistic scumbag and, what made it even worse, he took me to a restaurant Jake used to take me too . . ." I pause realizing he has no clue who Jake was. "Oh, Jake was my fiancé, he died two years ago."

"I'm sorry to hear that." And there's the pity look. The one everyone gives me when I tell them about Jake. I hate that look.

"Thanks. So anyway, as I sat there listening to him talk about his house in the Hamptons and how much money he makes, I kept having these memories of me and Jake sitting at our favorite booth flash through my head, and I started to have a panic attack. I excused myself saying I was going to the bathroom then ducked out through the kitchen."

"Are you serious? You just bolted?" Brian lets out a hardy laugh.

"And I never looked back," I replied

"That is fucking hilarious. What did you do after that?"

"I went home and got completely hammered while looking through old photo albums of Jake and me. And in a moment of drunken clarity I decided it was time to move. Get a fresh start to a place where every time I turn a corner it wouldn't remind me of Jake. So I stumbled into Jake's office where he had this huge map of the U.S. up on the wall behind his desk and grabbed one of the darts from his dartboard hidden behind his office door. I stood on unsteady feet in front of his desk and, through drunken blurry eyes; I threw the dart then proceeded to pass out on the floor before I could see where it had landed."

Brian bursts into laughter almost falling over onto the ground. "Now you're just fucking with me, aren't you?"

"No, this actually happened. I told you it was crazy."

"It's not crazy, but it is by far the most fascinating story I've ever heard."

"The next morning I woke up, still on the floor. My head was pounding and I had faint memories of what had happened the night before. I peeled myself up off the floor and walked over to the map where the dart was smack dab in the middle of Seattle."

"So you moved to Seattle because you drunkenly threw a dart at a map?" His eyebrow cocks up curiously at me. "Maybe it is slightly crazy but ballsy as hell. It takes guts to move to a new city where you know absolutely no one. So I definitely commend you for taking the leap."

"Um . . . thanks. But it wasn't the only reason. When I was a kid my dad brought my brother and me to visit after my mom passed away. This city brought me such happiness that I thought maybe the dart was guiding me back here. And maybe fate had a purpose for me here."

I know it's crazy, but I believe that fate was telling me I was meant to be here. For what, I still have no clue, but I know fate will reveal its plan for me when it's the right time. Like it did when I met Jake.

"So what did your job say after you decided to up and quit?"

"That wasn't an issue. I write books and I can do that anywhere," I reply, watching Brian adjusting bookshelves up against the wall. I pull my lip between my teeth, watching his muscles flex under his shirt.

"Oh really, what kind of books do you write?" he asks.

"I write dark, erotic novels. Well, at least I used to." I let out a small sigh, just thinking about the blank pages sitting on my laptop. Even with my publisher giving me an extension on my new novel, I still haven't been able to write a damn word.

"What do you mean used to?" Brian walks into the kitchen and grabs a beer from the fridge. He leans back against the counter, twisting off the cap and takes a sip.

"Well, I found my muse after I met my fiancé and, after he died, I lost her voice."

"It's understandable. You lost someone you cared about, it can be hard to focus after something like that."

"True, but I thought after two years I'd be able to start writing again. I guess it's hard to write dirty filthy smut when I'm not getting any."

"Wait, are you telling me you haven't had sex in two years?" His eyes widen in disbelief.

"Yes, and I have already heard how insane that is from Lucky, so you can just keep your trap shut on the issue."

Brian threw his hands up in surrender. "I will just say this. If you need a little inspiration in this department, I'm more than happy to volunteer my services. Wouldn't want to let your fans down."

"Oh, so this is just for my fans, huh? Not because you want to get into my pants?" I cross my arms in front of me, giving him a sideways glance.

"Well, that too, but mainly for your fans." He chuckles.

"As tempting as that offer is, I'm gonna pass." I turn my back to him and start back to work on making my meatballs. Before I can take the pot off the stove, I feel the heat from his body right behind me. His hands rest on either side of the counter, locking me in his trap. My breathing shallows and my heart begins to beat faster.

"Are you sure?" he asks. His breath hot against my ear. I

want to say yes so badly, but I'm not ready for this. Not until I can contain all these wild emotions I'm feeling for Brian. I turn around in his arms. My breath hitches when I meet his dark gaze.

"Brian, I just . . ." I drop my eyes away from his. But his hand slips under my chin and he lifts my eyes back to his.

"Hey, what's going on?" he asks with sincerity in his voice.

"For the past two years I've been completely numb inside. I've basically been walking around like a zombie. But since that night at your door I've had a flood of emotions hit me like a fucking tidal wave. At first I wanted to hate you because you were right, I was jealous that whoever that girl was got to sleep with you and I didn't." Brian's lips seal in a thin line, trying to hide an 'I told you so' smile. "But I couldn't admit that because you were just a voice through my wall at the time, and I felt embarrassed for wanting someone whose face I hadn't even seen. And now, you're a flesh and blood man, who one minute thinks I'm a crazy bitch then the next is telling me he wants to fuck me. My head is spinning trying to keep up and, on top of all that, I'm struggling with all these feelings for you and feeling this wave of guilt like I'm leaving Jake's memory behind, well, I'm just a huge mess," I say trying fight back the tears welling up in my eyes.

Brian pulls me into his arms. "I'm so sorry, Brooke. I've been utterly selfish in this whole thing. I should be trying to be a friend to you, not trying to sleep with you. I'm so sorry."

"You don't have to be sorry." I slide my arms around him, resting my head against his chest just above his heart. I haven't been held like this by anyone that wasn't my brother in too damn long. His arms feel so good around me and he smells fantastic.

"Yes, I do. I promise to lay off the sexual innuendos. I can't promise they won't come out from time to time because you're just so damn sexy, and I can't help myself, but I'll ease back. Okay?" he asks running his fingers through my hair.

"Okay." I smile to myself. "Dinner is ready. Would you like to hang out and watch a movie with me tonight? I could use the company. I promise to turn off my sexy." I giggle softly, looking up at him.

"I would love to. And that's impossible," he replies with a wink.

⋆ ⋆ ⋆

"Damn Brooke, dinner was so damn good," Brian calls out from the living room. He's laying back on the couch, his feet up on the coffee table and he's rubbing his hand on his stomach and sighing happily.

"I'm glad you liked it. It was kind of nice cooking for someone else for a change." I smile, handing him a beer and taking my seat next to him on the couch. "So what movie did you pick?"

"Empire Strikes Back," he replies, pushing play on my Apple TV.

"Ooh, I love that movie. It's by far my favorite out of the series."

"Wow! You can cook, bake, and you love Star Wars? You're making it hard not to want to jump your bones right now." He chuckles, taking a sip of his beer.

"I bet it's hard." I give him a sideways glance as I take a sip of my wine.

"You're killing me, Brooke," he says shaking his head.

"I'm sorry, how about we change the subject. So did you always want to be a cop?"

"My dad was a cop, my grandfather was a cop, and my aunts on my dad's side are cops. So it's kind of in my DNA. Seeing my dad every morning dressed in his uniform and keeping the streets safe made me want to follow in his footsteps."

"I bet he's very proud of you."

I see Brian's face drop, his whole demeanor shifting. "I don't really know if he is or not. He died when I was six."

My heart breaks a little for him, I know how it feels to lose a parent. "I'm so sorry, Brian. I understand how you feel, I lost my mom when I was eight. I always struggle with if she would be proud of how I turned out. But I am sure your dad is proud of you."

"Thanks, and I'm sure your mom is proud of you for going after your dream of writing." He gives me a warm smile.

As we sit watching the movie, I somehow manage to creep closer and closer to Brian until I'm cuddled up next him, and his arm is around me. It feels so good to have someone to cuddle with. I didn't realize how much I've missed it.

We stayed this way through the entire movie until we both ended up falling asleep in each other's arms.

CHAPTER NINE

Brian

"COME ON LADY, JUST PICK a book already," I groan, standing in the back of Barnes and Noble. Me, in a bookstore . . . not something you see every day; my mother would be so proud. The last time I stepped into a book store willingly was college. Reading has never been very high on my list of priorities, but when Brooke mentioned that she writes books for a living, it peeked my curiosity. So here I am, hiding in the mysteries section, waiting for the woman in the Romance section to fucking pick a book already. I swear she's looked at every book twice.

I go to peek around the corner when a sales woman passes by and asks if I need any help finding anything. I grab a random book off the end cap and tell her I'm good. She politely smiles then turns and walks away and, just as she passes, the woman in the romance section finally leaves. I glance from side to side making sure the coast is clear, then slowly step around the corner. I walk down the row of shelves and I feel completely out of my element, lost in a sea of lady porn. God help me if Ryder ever knew I came in here and bought a romance novel. The wrath of shit I would get from him would last for years.

Scanning each shelf, I look for the M's, stopping dead in my tracks when I spot the shelf dedicated to Brooke's books.

There has to be at least a dozen of them, and all of them filled with her words. I run my fingers over each one trying to decide which I should get. One title sticks out to me the most, 'Sins of the Heart.' I pull it off the shelf and read the synopsis on the back, when I get to the end, I see a small picture of Brooke in the bottom left corner. She looks so young and innocent. Even in picture form her deep blue eyes sear into me. I clutch the book to my chest and walk the maze of bookshelves back up to the front to the cashier.

As I set the book down on the counter, the woman standing behind the cash register gives me a puzzled look over the rim of her purple glasses. "Gift for your girlfriend?" she asks politely.

"No, it's for me. I know the author, and I just wanted to check out her books," I reply.

Her face lights up when I mention that I know Brooke. "You are so lucky to know her. I met her three years ago at a signing event in New York, she is the sweetest and by far one of my favorite authors. You picked one of her best books. You won't be able to put it down." She smiles handing me my receipt.

I take the slip of paper from her hand and thank her before grabbing my book and walking out of the store. I guess I'm not the only one whose life Brooke has touched.

* * *

Lola's barking pulls me back into reality and that's when I hear the knocking on my door. I glance over at the clock by my bed and, shit, it's already after six. I got home from the book store and sat down to read just a couple chapters of Brooke's book before she came over for dinner, and I ended up reading for over three hours. The woman at the book store was right, I couldn't put the book down. The way Brooke writes captured me so fiercely, every word sucked me in deeper and deeper. Making me crave her words. Even now, as I set the book down on my nightstand, I want to read more.

I walk through the living to the front door. Sliding back the chain I open the door to a smiling Brooke holding two brown paper bags of food. Just seeing her face makes my entire day better.

"I brought Thai food from that little place just down the block from our building." She steps inside and heads straight for the kitchen with Lola right on her heels. She sets down the bags of food then proceeds to grab a couple plates out of the cabinet and some silverware from the drawer, making herself right at home. She looks good in my apartment.

"Thank you for dinner," I say stepping behind her. I slide a hand along her lower back, causing a chill to run down her spine as I reach for the handle on the fridge to grab us a couple beers. I can't help but find little ways to touch her. I love the feeling of her soft curves under my hands. I might even keep her up late watching movies just so she will fall asleep curled up next to me, and I can wake up with her in my arms. I love the way she feels and the way her body just melds perfectly with mine.

"It's the least I could do since you bought dinner the last two nights and didn't mind me drooling on you while I slept," she says, pressing her back against my hand, like she doesn't want me to move it. "So what movie did you pick?"

"I was thinking tonight we could watch The Walking Dead. I haven't seen any of the episodes yet," I suggest.

"You just want to watch that so I will get scared and cuddle up next to you. Don't think I don't know what you are doing, Officer Gamble. I'm on to your games." She looks over her shoulder at me, giving me a sideways glance. I can't even fight back the smile tugging at my lips. She might be on to my little game, but it's not going to stop me from keeping her as close to me as possible.

"What can I say, I like having you around," I admit.

Her expression softens into a sweet little grin. "I like hanging out with you too." It makes my heart sore to hear her say that.

She turns around and hands me a plate of food. "If we are going to stay up all night watching The Walking Dead, we should have a picnic in your bed. Your couch is comfy but it's giving me a kink in my neck."

"Now you're just playing with fire. No woman I have ever brought into my bed has ever not had sex with me."

She gives me a cocky grin. "Looks like I will be the first." She turns and sashays toward my bedroom.

Between watching her ass in her tight yoga pants and the idea of her in my bed I'm hard. Down boy, I say to myself as I adjust my dick. I follow Brooke to my room and find her sitting in the middle of my bed holding her book up.

"You're reading my book?" She looks at me with a stunned expression.

"I was curious and wanted to see what you wrote." I set my plate of food on the nightstand and join her on the bed.

"So what did you think?" she asks.

"To be honest, I couldn't put it down. You're an amazing writer, Brooke. And you have one dirty fucking mind for someone who looks as innocent as you."

"It's always the innocent ones who have the dirtiest minds." She winks at me.

I lean into her ear. Her sweet scent filling my senses is only adding to the internal struggle my dick and my brain are currently having. "I don't think you are as innocent as you look," I whisper.

"You have no idea," she whispers back. Her words make my dick twitch inside my boxers. She is fucking killing me.

"You better be careful, Ace. You're in my bed and there is

nothing to keep me from cuffing you to the head board and reenacting all the dirty shit I read about in that filthy book of yours." I keep my tone dark and even, letting her know just how fucking serious I am. She keeps fucking teasing me, and I won't hesitate for a second to tear her out of her clothes and claim every inch of her as mine.

Her breathing shallows and a soft moan slips from her lips. I can smell how turned on she is right now. Just one kiss. One touch of my lips to her neck and she would submit to me. Instead of watching the undead take down the living, we could be spending the night devouring each other.

I lean in closer, my lips just centimeters away from the delicate skin of her neck, but before I can get any further, her hands press against my chest pushing me away. "You almost had me there, Brian. Nice try." She laughs, turning away from me to scoop Lola up into her lap. She's thinks I'm just messing with her but I'm not. I want her so bad right now I can barely see straight.

I reach over to the nightstand and grab the TV remote. Silently hoping watching people get their guts ripped out will help calm the beast in my pants. I don't know how much longer I can keep up this *just friend* bullshit.

CHAPTER TEN

Brooke

THE SUN THAT IS CREEPING in through the sheer curtains hanging over my living room windows stirs me awake. I find myself wrapped in a warm blanket of Brian on my couch and it feels like heaven. For the past few weeks this has become our routine. Dinner, Netflix, and cuddling on the couch until we both fall asleep. After the initial awkwardness, being with Brian has been easy and comforting. We were fast becoming friends and, Lucy was right, Brian wasn't the asshole I'd painted him to be when we first met. He's funny and sweet and I love spending time with him. I actually find myself missing him when he's working.

As much as we try to stay away from topics that lead to sex. It didn't matter, the most mundane of topics would turn sexual. But it actually feels good to flirt a little. Plus, it's fun to watch Brian squirm. Brian is doing his best to steer the conversions to new topics, even though I know it's killing him not to be able to rip me out of my clothes. It's sweet that he is trying to be a good boy even though I know he wants to be bad. Most of the time I wish he would give into the temptation and fuck me.

I snuggle in closer to Brian's chest, listening to his heartbeat and breathing in his manly scent. I wish we could stay like this forever. It's been so long since I'd slept in the arms of a man, I had forgotten how good it could feel. I feel safe and at home in his arms. I'm about to close my eyes again when I hear my phone start ringing from the kitchen. I reluctantly pull out of Brian's arms and climb off the couch. Walking over to the counter, I see Lucky's face on my phone.

"Listen up bitch," she snarls as soon as I answer.

"Good morning to you too, Lucky."

"Look, Lucy and I are done with you putting us aside so you and Brian can bang and build furniture and do God knows what else every night."

"Not like it's any of your business, but Brian and I are not banging," I reply. Sounds like someone woke up on the wrong side of the stripper pole.

"I don't care. Tonight your ass is coming out with Lucy and me. Girls only."

"Lucky, I don't—"

"Sorry sweet cheeks, but you don't get a say in this. Lucy is going to pick you up at nine, then you guys are going to meet me at the club, where we're going to get sloppy. Make sure you wear something slutty and bring plenty of ones."

Before I can say a single word, Lucky hangs up on me. Well, I guess I'm going out tonight. But she's right, I've been spending a lot of time with Brian and neglecting them. It might be fun to go out with Lucy and maybe finally get the story of why Lucky strips.

I set my phone down on the counter and start in on making a fresh pot of coffee.

"Good morning."

I hear Brian's sleepy voice come from behind me as I press start on my coffee pot. Turning around, I spot him sliding onto one of the barstools. His hair is messy and spiked up on one side. Sleepy Brian looks positively cute.

"Good morning," I say returning his sleepy smile.

"So who was on the phone?"

"Lucky. Seems her and Lucy are mad that I've been spending all my time with you lately. So they're taking me out for a girls only thing tonight at the Blue Moon Club."

He lets out a low sigh. "I guess they can have you for one night," he teases. "Works out anyway, Ryder pissed off the Captain, and now we're stuck with DUI checkpoint duty tonight."

"Why does that not surprise me?" I giggle softly, shaking my head. After hearing all the stories of Brian and Ryder's early days, I'm amazed they haven't been kicked off the force yet.

"They don't call us double trouble for nothing. Although I think I'd rather be doing checkpoint duty than go out for a night with Lucky. I'll warn you now, Lucky is fucking crazy when she drinks."

"I think I can handle her and can always taze her if she gets too out of line." I grin pouring our coffee.

"Now that . . . I would pay to see." He chuckles taking his mug from my hand. "Try not to have too much fun without me." He flashes me his sad puppy dog eyes.

I walk around the counter and slide my arms around Brian's neck. "I'll do my best, but I'll give you a little something to help keep you company tonight while you're at work."

"Oh, a naked selfie?" Brian replies, grinning from ear to ear and wiggling his eyebrows at me.

See? Always turns sexual with us.

"You're funny. But no." I reach over to my bag, grab my notebook, and hand it to him. "I started writing again a couple days ago. I think having you around has helped me clear out the fog. I wanted you to be the first to read the few chapters I've written."

"Brooke, that's fantastic. See I told you, you'd find your

voice again." He smiles, opening the cover. "Are you sure you want me to read this? Wouldn't you rather have Lucy see it?"

"You helped me find my muse again, so who better than you to read it first," I reply, giving him a confident smile. For months, I'd been struggling with writing this book, but stepping away from it and spending time with Brian cleared my head and the words started flowing again.

"Well, I'm honored."

"Good. I hope you like it." I give him a quick peck on the cheek. "I better go take a shower, and you better get back to Lola, I bet she misses you."

"Lola can wait a little bit longer while I help you in the shower."

"Go back home and take care of your dog and the morning wood that was poking me in the back earlier. You can think about me all hot, soapy, and naked in the shower." I wink. As I turn to head back to my bedroom, I feel Brian's hand slap against my ass, forcing out a yelp.

"Well, that was nice but next time put some muscle behind it," I tease.

"You're fucking killing me, Ace."

I grin to myself as I walk into my bedroom.

CHAPTER ELEVEN

Brian

THE ALARM ON MY PHONE goes off, jolting me awake. With tired eyes, I reach for the screeching siren on my nightstand and hit snooze. That's when I notice I have a new email from Brooke, she's sent me more pages from the book she's been working on. She must have been writing all day. I immediately sit up in bed, rubbing my tired eyes before reaching over to grab my laptop off my nightstand. I haven't been this excited to read a book in, well . . . ever. The only books I read these days are police procedure manuals. Since I picked up Brooke's books I haven't been able to put them down. I have every one of her books, and I feel honored that she is letting me read her newest project.

I rest back against the pillows and open up my laptop. The last point in the story, the main characters, Mark and Sophie, were about to reveal their true feelings for one another. I don't know why, but this story reminds me of Brooke and me. Two lost souls finding each other after being alone for so long. It almost feels like she's using this book to tell me her true feelings for me.

Ten pages in and my dick is standing at full attention, and my imagination is running wild. Mark has Sophie pinned to his bed, his face buried between her legs, tongue licking from clit to ass. Sophie is clawing at the sheets, screaming out her pleasure. Who knew my seemingly sweet innocent neighbor had such a dirty mind. Reading her beautiful and dirty words all I can imagine is that I'm Mark and Brooke is Sophie. Soon the words on my computer screen fade away and I can see Brooke slowly crawling up my bed. She is naked and the soft light from the setting sun is making her alabaster skin glow. Her full heavy tits gently sway as she moves further up the bed. Her hand reaches up grabbing the edge of the sheet, slowly pulling it down. Her warm tongue glides along her luscious lips as my erection comes into view.

She lowers herself over me, letting my dick slide between her big tits then down the rest of her body until he's nestled between her wet pussy lips. I can feel the gentle pulse of her clit against my cock and it makes me even more hungry for a taste of her.

"Tell me how much you want me, Brian. I need to hear it. Tell me. Tell me."

She chants over and over until her voice and her image fade away, and I'm alone in my bed once again. I know I promised to just be friends, but I can't be friends with Brooke anymore. My feelings are growing stronger with every minute we are together. I'm falling for her hard, and it's time I man up and tell her how I'm feeling.

CHAPTER TWELVE

Brooke

LUCY WAS AT MY DOOR promptly at nine, and as per Lucky's request, I was dressed in my sluttiest dress. A backless black number with a slit down the front that stops just below my navel. I've left my dark brown hair down in loose curls. I went for smoky dark eye makeup and ruby red lipstick and, to top it all off, I'm wearing my favorite black Louboutin's with the little spikes. I kind of wished Brian was home before I left so I could torture him just a little with my outfit.

Lucy stayed relatively quiet during the cab ride to the club. Which means I was probably going to get tag teamed by my girls about what was going on with me and Brian. But there wasn't much to tell, at least not yet. Brian and I are just friends, nothing more. At least that's what I keep telling myself even though I know we both want nothing more than to ravage each other's naked bodies.

We pull up to the club just after nine. The Blue Moon from the outside looks like an old brick paper factory. It's within walking distance from Safeco Field and Century Link Stadium. Nothing goes better with baseball and football like boobs and booze. We climb out of the cab then head inside. The front lobby is surprisingly plain. There's just a small glass counter where a big beast of a bouncer sits checking ID's, but once we step through the black velvet curtains, it's like we're in an entirely new building.

From the outside, I was expecting it to be seedy and creepy, but it's actually a pretty high-class club. Kind of like the ones I'd been to in Vegas with Jake. The main club area is dimly lit with soft blue lighting. To the left of the main stage is the bar and the kitchen. The wall to the right is flanked with blue leather booths. And the main stage stands in the center of the room. It's a round mahogany stage with a long silver stripper pole, right in the center, with stools placed all around it.

Lucy and I head straight for the bar and order our drinks, gin and tonic for her and whiskey neat for me. The club's pretty dead except for what looks like a couple of regulars that are seated at the far edge of the bar, watching the end of the Seahawks game on the television hanging behind the bar. Lucy and I grab our drinks and make our way to the main stage just as the DJ announces Lucky is up next. We pick two of the blue leather stools closest to the middle and lay out a row of dollar bills in front of us.

The music starts and Lucky steps out on stage and I almost don't recognize her. When I've seen her at the coffee shop or at Lucy's house she's always dressed pretty casual with minimal makeup and her blonde hair's usually pulled up into a messy bun on top of her head. Here she's dressed in a black lacy corset with a matching thong. Her makeup is dark, she even has fake lashes, and her hair is down with big curls that frame her perky breasts.

Lucky spots us immediately and flashes a little wink as she steps up to the pole. I lean over to Lucy. "Have you seen Lucky dance before?"

"The last time I was here was when Lucky had just moved back from San Francisco. Normally, when I get a mom's night out, I don't want to spend it in a strip club, but Lucky had to work tonight so here we are."

Just as we turn back to watch Lucky, she's beginning to crawl toward us. She pushes aside our money and comes to the edge of the stage eyeing me up and down then flashing me an approving smile before burying her face between my breasts.

"Oh, hey there!" I giggle, as Lucky motor boats me.

"Hey sexy," she replies. "You got some nice tits there, Brooke." She turns onto her back and rests her head back on my boobs.

"Thanks." I grin, sliding a dollar down between her cleavage.

"So, what's going on between you and Brian?"

Okay, well, looks like the pleasantries are over and we're cutting right to the chase. Lucky sits back up, rolls onto her stomach, and slowly curls her legs up and over her head, resting her feet flat on the stage by her head. Damn, she's fucking flexible. No wonder she's the most popular stripper here.

"Brian and I are just friends. We like hanging out with each other," I say, trying to brush them off.

"If you aren't fucking, what the hell are you guys doing every night?" Lucky asks, unclasping her corset revealing her full creamy breasts.

"Well, first off, nice rack." I wink. "Second, Brian has been helping me get settled into my apartment. We take turns making dinner and we have these amazing long talks. Then, usually end the night watching Netflix."

"Well, that sounds completely boring."

"Don't listen to her, Brooke," Lucy chimes in. "What that sounds like is the old Brian is resurfacing."

"What do you mean by the old Brian?" I ask curiously.

"Brian wasn't always the womanizing pain in the ass you first met. He once had dreams of getting married and having kids. He almost came close—"

"Until that cunt bag got her nasty claws into him and ripped his fucking heart out," Lucky snarls.

"Jillian was a piece of work. They met at the police academy six years ago. She seemed completely normal until after graduation, then everything turned into one big competition with her. She had to be the best at everything, and she didn't care how or who she hurt to get it."

"She even went as far as sleeping with their captain in Brian's bed. He walked in on them one night," Lucky replies then moves down the stage to show her regulars some love.

"Oh my God! What a bitch." How could anyone do that to someone like Brian? Sure, he can be a pain in the ass sometimes, but he doesn't deserve that kind of heartbreak.

"That's putting it mildly. She got into his fucking head, telling him he was a shitty cop and that he would never last on the force. But she was just jealous because Brian is the best damn cop the Seattle PD has, she just projected her own insecurities onto him instead of dealing with her problems." Lucy pauses, taking a sip of her cocktail.

"What happened after he caught them?"

"He walked out and the next day he requested a transfer to a new precinct. He hasn't seen her since, which is for the best, but the bitch still manages to fuck with his head. Which is why he's spent the past four years drinking and fucking anything with tits to help numb the pain. Brian isn't really that guy, deep down he's a good guy who wants to believe in love again. Which is why I'm happy to see he's actually the Brian I remember. The sweet guy who'd give you the shirt off his back if you needed it. The guy who's a friend to a woman who he desperately wants to sleep with but knows right now just needs his friendship." She flashes me a little wink.

I know she's talking about me. I may be helping him change and find himself again, but he's changing me too. I haven't felt this happy in such a long time and it's because of him. If what Lucy's saying is true, then maybe, just maybe, what we have is real.

"He's been a really good friend. He's just so easy to be around. I feel comfortable with him and can tell him anything and he doesn't judge me. But . . ." My voice begins to fade and trail off.

"But what?" Lucy asks.

"But why do I feel guilty? Like I'm somehow cheating on Jake."

Lucy slides her hand over mine, giving me a comforting smile. "After Colton died I felt exactly the way you are now, but I realized Colton wouldn't want me to stop living just because he was gone, and I believe with all my heart Jake wouldn't want that for you either. If Brian makes you happy, then I know Jake would be thrilled that you found someone who makes you feel alive again."

She was right. One thing that Jake taught me was to never give up on life, to go out and find what makes me happy and, right now, Brian was doing just that.

"Look, just take things slow with Brian. You've both been through so much, it might be good that you guys be friends for a while. The other stuff can come later when you're both are ready." She smiles at me again.

"You're right, Lucy. You always know just what to say," I say returning her smile.

"That's because I'm awesome. Now, what do you say we stop with the heavy talk and have some fucking fun?"

"Hell yes. Let's do this."

We down the last of our drinks and wave down the waitress to order a few shots of tequila.

CHAPTER THIRTEEN

Brian

"DAMN I COULD USE A fucking cocktail after that bullshit shift." Ryder huffs, sitting down next to me on the bench in the locker room. DUI checkpoint duty is always left for the morons that pissed off the Captain, so needless to say it's a shift Ryder and I are far too familiar with.

"Wanna come over for a beer?"

"Nah, I'm good. I need to get home to Lola."

Ryder's glance narrows at me. "Lola, huh? More like you want to get back to Brooke."

I hate it when he can see right through me. But he's right, I am eager to see Brooke and tell her how much I love the pages of her new book and, hell, I just want to see her beautiful smiling face again. Most importantly . . . I'm ready to tell her I want to be with her.

"What's going on with you two?"

"We're just hanging out. I'm trying to be the friend she needs right now." I pull my shirt on over my head. "I'm trying my hardest to just be friends, but the more time I spend with her, getting to know her, it makes me want her even more," I admit

"But . . ." Ryder challenges.

"But nothing, she's so fucking amazing. She is funny and sweet . . . smart as a fucking whip. I feel so damn happy when I'm around her." I can't fight back the smile tugging at my lips.

"You're really falling for this girl, aren't you?"

"I think I am, but it's scaring the shit out of me. I haven't felt this way about a woman since Jillian, and you saw how that turned out."

"Yeah, but Brooke is not like Jillian. Brooke is a kindhearted, sweet human being. She's the type of girl that will have your back instead of trying to stick a knife in it. If you want to be with her, you have to tell her. Don't make the same mistake I did." He drops his head with a sigh, stuffing his uniform into his gym bag.

Five years ago Ryder had his chance to finally tell Lucky that he was in love with her, but the pussy chickened out. She ran off to San Francisco where she met her douchebag ex, Jackson, who still manages to weasel back into her life every so often. Ryder's been in love with Lucky since he was five. But Lucky has always made it clear that she only wants to be friends with him, claiming it was because she didn't want to lose their friendship. But in my opinion, it was her lame excuse for not wanting to be happy for once in her life. I love Lucky like a sister, but she's a fucking moron, and one day he's going to give up on chasing her and will move on to someone who wants a nice guy like Ryder.

"It's time for you to start taking some of your own advice and finally get your girl. If Brooke can put up with your moody ass, then she's a fucking winner, and you need to go get her before someone else does."

"How does a dumb ass like you always know what to say?"

"I have my moments." He laughs flinging his gym bag over his shoulder. "I'm outta here, remember what I said." He starts to walk toward the door then pauses and looks back at me. "It's good to have you back."

"What does that mean?" I ask.

"Since Brooke came into your life it's like the old Brian is back. As much fun as it was tearing it up with you every night at the bar, I'm glad this Brian is back."

* * *

The old Brian. Those words stuck in my head as I drove home. I've forgotten who that even is. That Brian believed in love, believed there was good in everyone. That Brian was willing to lay everything on the line, even take a bullet for the woman he loved. That version of me had long since died. At least, that's what I use to think.

I step out of the elevator and start walking toward my apartment, but I stop in front of Brooke's door. It's three in the morning and she's probably asleep, but that doesn't keep me from knocking and wanting to see her. I wait a few moments but no answer. I reluctantly head over to my door and as I unlock the deadbolt I hear a familiar laugh coming from behind me. I turn around in time to see Brooke and Lucy walking toward me.

As soon as Brooke spots me her face lights up like a kid in a candy store. Her beautiful blue eyes sparkling with excitement to see me. And damn if it doesn't feel good.

"Hi Brian," she shouts, her words slightly slurred.

"Hey, Brooke. I see you ladies had fun tonight." I eye Brooke up and down. She looks fucking hot in her curve-hugging dress and damn that slit in the front. I'm amazed it can keep her tits from falling out.

"This one more so," Lucy says, looking flustered and exhausted which is usually how everyone looks after a night with Lucky. "Can you help get her into her apartment? Lucky is down in the cab hitting on the poor cab driver."

"I would be happy to." She hands me Brooke's shoes and a big bag of tacos. She says goodnight to Brooke and mouths a thank you to me before she heads back down the stairs.

I slide my arm around Brooke's waist helping to steady her wobbly legs. "Wow Brooke, did you drink an entire barrel of tequila? Nobody light a match," I tease.

"You're so funny Brian," she says, pinching my cheeks between her fingers.

Drunk Brooke is fucking adorable. I open the door of my apartment thinking it's better she not be alone right now. I help her sit down at the kitchen table and hand her a bag of tacos then head to the kitchen to get her some water. "Did you have fun tonight?"

"I had a freaking blast. And you were right, Lucky is fucking crazy but fun, though," she slurs, taking a big bite of her taco. "As much fun as it was, I missed you."

I smile to myself. She fucking missed me. I wonder what else I can get her to admit to in her drunken state. "You did, huh?"

She nods yes and continues to demolish her taco. "Well, I missed you too," I admit.

"You did?" She grins from ear to ear.

"I miss you when you're not around."

"How did I get so lucky to make a friend like you, Brian?"

"You came knocking on my door."

She takes out another taco from her bag and barely gets the wrapper off by the time it hits her mouth. I set her glass of water down on the table then I take a seat across the table from her. I watch quietly while she eats her food, her moans almost sexual as she chews.

"God, I fucking love tacos," she mumbles.

"Do you want me to leave you and your tacos alone?" I ask stifling a chuckle.

"You're such a comedian, Brian." She giggles. "You know what would make these even better?"

"Hot sauce?" I say cocking an eyebrow up at her.

Brooke gets up from her chair and walks over to me then straddles my lap. I get a full view of the slit in front of her dress. Her gorgeous tits almost begging for my lips to be all over them. "They would be better if I was eating them while riding this throne of a jaw of yours." She runs her fingers along my jaw and over my lips. She pulls her lip between her teeth, and I can hear her breath deepen as she imagines what it would feel like to have my face buried between her thighs. I've imagined it a million times myself.

"I'm tired of fighting it," she finally speaks and my heart leaps into my chest. I pray she says what I've been dying to hear since I met her.

"Tired of fighting what?" I ask in a whispered tone.

"I'm tired of fighting with how much I want you. Brian, I want you to make love to me. I know you want to; I can feel it in the way you look at me." Her hips gently roll against the growing hard-on in my pants. She reaches behind her neck and starts to unhook her dress. But I grab her hands, stopping her.

It's been two years since she'd felt the touch of a man. Two years since she's let anyone make love to her. I knew the moment she first uttered the words that I wanted to be the first man to touch her, to kiss her, to be inside her. I want to be the first man to make her come undone. But not like this. I don't want her to regret the first time we have sex.

"Not like this Brooke." I bring her hands back down, keeping them in mine.

"Come on Brian, I really want this," she pleads, looking at me with disappointment in her eyes.

"I know you do and so do I, but when I fuck you for the first time, I want you sober. I want you to remember every caress of my hands, every kiss from my lips, every slow lick of my tongue across your pretty little pussy. I especially want you to know that the ache you'll be feeling days after we fuck is because of me."

Brooke sucks in a ragged breath and her eyes begin to flutter. The next thing I know her body goes limp and she passes out against my chest. All I can do is shake my head. Seems about right.

I scoop Brooke up into my arms and carry her to my bed and carefully lay her down. I gently sweep her hair to the side and lean in to softly kiss her forehead. I feel slightly relieved that she feels the same way about me. I just hope she doesn't change her mind once she sobers up. I cover her up with my blanket and as I do, Lola jumps up onto the bed and curls up next to Brooke.

"You like her, huh?"

Lola lets out an agreeing bark.

"I like her too."

CHAPTER FOURTEEN

Brooke

I WAKE UP TO A warm tongue licking my face. Cracking open an eye, I see Lola sitting over me and begin to wonder how I ended up at Brian's. Sitting up, I pull Lola into my arms, petting her behind her ears. "Hey, where's your daddy?" I scan Brian's bedroom trying to figure out what happened after I left the club. The last thing I remember is doing shots. Well, more like Lucky pouring tequila down my throat. Which explains the pounding headache.

"Good morning sleepyhead."

I look up and see Brian walking into the room. He's dressed in a white T-shirt and a pair of gray sweatpants that hang low on his hips and, God help me, I can see an impression of his cock through the fabric. He strides over to me, holding a glass of water in one hand and a bottle of Tylenol in the other.

"Good morning, and how did I end up in your bed last night?" I ask, taking the water and popping a couple of Tylenol tablets into my mouth. "I'm dressed and I still have my panties on, so I'm assuming we didn't have sex last night."

"It wasn't for a lack of trying on your end. But I make it a point not to sleep with a woman who is unconscious. I'm a gentleman that way." He smiles, sitting on the edge of the bed.

"You don't remember anything from last night?"

Oh God, this is exactly why I don't drink tequila anymore. It turns me into a horny monster. I can't believe he put up with me last night. "It's like blurred images. The last thing I remember is sitting at the bar and Lucky was pouring tequila down my throat."

"That sounds like a Lucky thing to do." He chuckles.

"I'm sorry for anything I said or did last night. I haven't had that much to drink in a long time. Thank you for taking care of me." I shyly grin, feeling completely embarrassed about my actions.

"I couldn't leave you alone. You were pretty far gone."

"Thank you, it means a lot to me that you were looking out for me." If Brian gets any sweeter, I'm not going to be able to resist ripping off his clothes and fucking his damn brains out.

"That's what friends do for each other." And that crooked smile makes an appearance. God, I love that smile. "You, by the way, have an odd fascination with tacos."

"Yeah, they're kind of my go-to drunk food. When I was still living in Boston, my brother came home to find me drunk sitting in the middle of our front lawn chowing down on deep-fried tacos."

I look up at Brian and get a flash of me sitting on his lap trying to take my dress off last night and, like a tidal wave, it all comes flashing back. In my drunken state, I was practically begging to have sex with him. Fucking Tequila. He probably thinks I'm even crazier now. I feel my cheeks burning hot, and the room seems to be getting warmer. I need to get out of here.

"I better go. I've worn out my welcome." I set Lola down on the bed and start to crawl out from under the blankets. "Thank you for taking care of me last night and thanks for the Tylenol."

"Please don't go." Brian grabs my hand stopping me. "There's something I need to talk to you about."

My heart begins to pound in my chest as another image of Brian telling me he wanted to fuck me flashes in my mind. His words ringing in my ears. "I want you to remember every caress of my hands, every kiss my lips." And oh God. "Every slow lick of my tongue across your pretty little pussy." And now my panties are feeling a bit damp.

"What did you want to talk about?" I ask.

"How about we talk after you take a shower and get some food in you. I'm making some omelets with bacon, and coffee." Damn it, he knows I can't resist coffee or bacon.

"But I don't have anything to change into."

"You can borrow one of my shirts." He gets up from the bed and disappears into his closet. He reappears holding his Seattle PD T-shirt. "Please stay." His

voice is pleading.

"Okay, I'll stay."

Brian's face relaxes and he gives me a gentle smile before he heads back out to the kitchen to finish making breakfast. I look over at Lola, who has her little head tilted to the side at me.

"He wants to be more than friends, huh?"

She lets out a yip of a bark.

"I do too, but I'm scared."

Lola climbs into my lap and nuzzles her face against my neck, like in her own way telling me not to be scared. I really want to be with Brian so badly, but I've only known him for a few weeks, and the first week I hated him. How can I be having such strong feelings for someone I barely know? And what about Jake and the guilt I'm having about leaving him behind.

Lola barks and then lets out a low growl.

"Okay, okay, I'll stop overthinking it."

I'm losing it. I'm talking to a dog about my love life. I climb out of bed and head to the bathroom. Starting the water in the shower, I let it warm up while I slip out of my dress then slide my panties off. I step into the shower and warm water washes over me. Grabbing a bottle of shampoo, I flip open the top, breathing in the fresh scent. It smells of him and, with that, my hesitations begin to fade away, and all that runs through my head is us on my couch sleeping in each other's arms. My new safe place. I remember Lucy's words from last night. I know Jake would want me to move on and be happy, and Brian makes me happy. So, whatever he has to say, I'm going to be open to it.

⋆ ⋆ ⋆

I finish up in the shower and try to tame my wet tangled locks. Wiping off the last of the smeared mascara from under my eyes before slipping back into my panties, I pull on Brian's shirt. I head out to the kitchen with Lola following not far behind me. I'm feeling refreshed and ready to talk with Brian.

Brian looks up from his phone just as I step into the kitchen, his face lighting up when he sees me. "Feeling better?" he asks as I take a seat at the table.

In front of me is a beautiful plate of food. A ham and cheese omelet with bacon and fresh fruit, orange juice, and coffee. He went all out.

"Much better. This looks positively delicious." I smile, taking a bite of my bacon. I look over at his spot and his plate is empty. "Aren't you having any?"

"I will after my shower. You just sit and enjoy." He pushes his chair back from the table. He starts to walk toward his bedroom, but pauses next to my chair and looks down at me. "I'm glad you decided to stay." He leans down and kisses the top of my head then turns and walks back to his bedroom. I'm glad I stayed too. It's time we finally talked about the feelings we are having for each other.

I dig into my breakfast and moan in pleasure at how good my omelet tastes. Damn, this man sure knows how to cook.

Just as I take my first sip of coffee, I hear Brian begin to sing in the shower. It sounds like he's singing 'Cherry Pie' by Warrant. Could he be any cuter?

A few minutes later I hear the water turn off and, just as I look up from now empty plate of food, I see Brian walk into his bedroom, drying his hair with his towel and he's completely naked. No towel around his waist, nothing. He must've forgotten he left the bedroom door open. I can't seem to pull my eyes away from him.

It's just a naked man, it's just a naked man. Take a deep breath Brooke. It's just a naked man. You've seen your share before. Just a naked man. I chant to myself, but who the hell am I kidding? That man has the most amazing body I've ever seen. Get it together Brooke, and for God sakes, stop staring you perv. Before I can peel my eyes away from him, he turns around and through the open bedroom door my eyes meet not so little Gamble.

"Fuck me," I whisper under my breath. Of course, he has a big, thick, beautiful cock. Explains all the screams of, "Oh God, I love your cock," I used to hear through my walls at night.

I squeeze my thighs together. My mind starts to wonder and I imagine what it would feel like to ride that big dick of his. To have him fill me completely. Lost in my thoughts, eyes still locked on Brian's gorgeous naked body, I don't notice that Brian is watching me.

"You see something you like there, Ace?"

I snap back into reality and can feel my face burning red. He wraps his towel around his waist and starts walking toward me. I stand up from the table and meet him halfway in the living room. My mind is reeling and my hormones are in overdrive. I wanted to stay just friends for as long as possible but my need for him, my need to feel him on top of me, under me, and inside of me is overtaking me. I think he can sense it too because the moment I step in front of him he slides his arm around my waist pulling me to him. I rest my hands against his chest. His skin is warm and wet and his muscles are toned and perfect.

"Brian . . ." He places his fingers over my mouth stopping me from saying another word.

"Brooke, I can't do this. I can't just be friends with you anymore. I can't keep fucking fighting how much I want you." He lets out a low growl from his chest. "Do you feel that Brooke?" He pulls me tighter against him and I can feel his desire for me pressing against my stomach. "This is what you do to me. It's what you've done to me since that night you showed up at my door. I want you so fucking badly I can barely breathe."

I pull my lip between my teeth. I'd known he wanted to fuck me, but I didn't realize that he was feeling the same frustrations I was.

"You're all I can think about. When I'm asleep, I'm dreaming of you. When I'm awake, I think about you, and fuck, when I jerk off it's you I see." He lets out a small ragged sigh. "So please put me out of my misery and tell me what your body already has. I need to hear it, please," he begs, his breath hot against my neck.

My heart is beating out of my chest, my panties soaked with my need for him. I can't deny it to myself or to him any longer. I need him more than I need air.

"I fucking need you, Brian."

Our lips come crashing together in a deep heated kiss, his tongue tracing along my lips, begging for entrance. My lips part and his greedy tongue devours me, tasting every inch of my mouth. We kiss like we need each other to breathe.

I pull away. Both of us are breathing hard and panting. "Take me to your bed," I murmur, pulling him back to my lips.

Brian lifts me up in his arms and wraps my legs around his

waist. He carries me into his bedroom and gently sets me down on his bed. He takes a step back and I sigh at the loss of his touch.

"Are you sure you're ready for this? Because once I start I won't be able to stop myself. I've wanted for this for too long."

"I want this more than anything." I pull off my shirt, tossing it to the floor. Grabbing Brian's hand, I pull him back to me and rip open his towel, letting it fall to the floor. "Make me feel alive again, Brian."

With that Brian tangles his fingers into my hair, pulling my head back. His hot mouth trailing down my neck, licking and sucking at my delicate skin. He lays me back on the bed and hooks his fingers under the lace of my panties and slides them down off my hips. He brings them up to his nose, breathing in my scent before tossing them over his shoulder. He looks down at me with dark hooded eyes, sending a delicious wave of pleasure down between my legs.

"You're so fucking beautiful," he says, crawling over me.

I can feel my whole body flush at his words. He dips down, kissing me softly. His rough fingers feeling gentle against my skin as he explores my body with his lips and hands. He trails feather light kisses down along my chest. Running his tongue between my breasts, he gently rolls my nipple between his nimble fingers while sucking the other into his mouth. His touch ignites a fire I thought had long since died.

He continues his exploration down my body, dipping his tongue into my belly button. He makes every nerve in my body tingle as he runs his tongue along my hips. His morning scruff tickles along my inner thigh while he leaves a trail of hot kisses. He rests my legs over his shoulders and lets out a primal growl when he sees how wet I am for him. I'm practically dripping wet with need.

My body nearly flies off the bed when his tongue gently

strokes along my slit. "Oh God, Brian," I softly moan. My hand drifts down to his head, fingers gripping his hair. Holding him in place.

He moves his tongue up and down my wet lips, working me open and, before I know it, his mouth is on me and his dangerously long tongue is pushing inside me. His face pressed between my legs, the sensation of his lips, his tongue, and his nose bumping against my clit is fucking mind blowing. It's been so long since someone has eaten me out this good that I know I won't last long. Brian grips my thighs keeping me steady as he begins shaking his head back and forth. His tongue tasting every inch of me.

"You taste so fucking good, Brooke," he growls. He spreads me open, rolling my throbbing bud between his fingers and blows a cool breeze of air along my hot flesh, and I almost fly off the bed.

He continues his sweet torture, sucking and licking until I'm writhing and bucking against his mouth. Brian pushes two of his long thick fingers deep inside me, slowing pumping them in and out. His mouth covering my clit, tongue flicking, teeth grazing, and all it takes is one last pump of his fingers and my orgasm rips through me, and I'm coming all over Brian's face.

As I start to come down from my high, a wave of emotion begins to wash over me and the tears begin to stream down my face. Brian crawls up me and his satisfied smile turns into a look of concern when he sees me crying.

"Brooke, are you okay?" He gently strokes my cheek.

"I'm fine," I reply giving him a reassuring smile. "These are happy tears. It's been so long since I've felt this good it's just a little overwhelming."

"Do you want to stop?" he asks, wiping the tears from my cheeks.

I grab his wrist, pulling his hand away. "Please don't stop. I want this Brian."

He places a gentle kiss on my lips then sits up and grabs a condom out of his nightstand. He tears open the foil and rolls the condom down his hard length. Climbing over me, covering my body with his, the weight of him on top of me feels phenomenal. I've missed feeling the heaviness of a man. He softly kisses my lips as he guides himself to my entrance and pushes just the tip inside me. He laces his fingers with mine and brings our hands above my head, then he presses his forehead against mine. His eyes locked on mine as he pushes further inside me until he's fully seated. We fit perfectly together, like we were made for each other.

He's slow at first, drawing out every thrust. Pulling out and waiting until I can no longer take the emptiness, then thrusts inside me again. Filling me completely. He keeps me in his gaze, watching every flicker of pleasure flash in my eyes and devouring every moan of ecstasy that slips from my lips. Each slow deep thrust makes me feel more and more alive.

"You feel so good, Brooke," he says in a hushed tone.

Wrapping my legs around Brian's waist, he lets out a low growl as he slips deeper inside me. As our bodies move together, I can feel that familiar fire building deep inside me.

"That's it beautiful, let me feel you come," he groans picking up his pace, and it's not long before he sends me flying over the edge, screaming his name. My pussy is throbbing, pulling him along with me. He moans and grunts as he comes, and they are the most beautiful sounds I've ever heard.

Brian collapses on top of me, nuzzling his face into my neck. Both of us breathing hard. I gently stroke his back and kiss the top of his head. I'm completely soaring. I'm feeling so alive and high on Brian.

God help me, I want more.

"Do you have to work today?"

"No, I'm off for the next couple days, why?" he asks peeking his head up.

I roll him onto his back keeping him firmly seated inside me. "Good because I'm not even close to having my fill of you."

CHAPTER FIFTEEN

Brian

I CRACK AN EYE OPEN to check the time on my alarm, nine a.m. Thanks to a very insatiable Brooke, I've only gotten four hours of sleep. But it was the best four hours of sleep I've had in years. I roll over ready to feel my girl in my arms.

My girl . . . Damn, if that doesn't sound good.

Had anyone told me a few months ago that I would let a woman sleepover at my apartment, let alone jump head first into a relationship with that woman, I would have told them they were a fucking idiot. But here I am, ready to take the leap with Brooke.

I reach out for Brooke, sadly finding her side empty and cold. I sit up looking around my room trying to find any sign of her. Could it be that yesterday was just a dream? No, it felt too damn real, and I can still smell her all over me. That's when it hits me, the fresh scent of bacon and maple syrup wafting in from the kitchen. I smile to myself as I climb out of bed and realize someone is surprising me with breakfast. I slip on a pair of boxers and walk out to the kitchen. I stop dead in my tracks when I spot Brooke lying naked on my kitchen table with a plate of what looks to be pancakes, eggs, and bacon sitting on her stomach and sliced strawberries placed ever so delicately over her nipples.

"Good morning, handsome." She grins, staying perfectly still.

"Good morning, Ace. Did you make me breakfast?"

"I sure did. I hope you like pancakes, eggs, bacon, and me." She softly giggles.

"You spoil me, Ace." I walk over to the table and lean over, taking one of the strawberry slices into my mouth. Giving her pretty pink nipple a nip before moving to the second berry, I love the squeals that escape from Brooke's lips. I grab my plate of food and take my seat right between her legs, and I can't help but lick my lips at the sight of her beautiful pussy. Her lips already glistening with her sweet juices. I've eaten my fair share of pussy, but nothing compares to Brooke. Just the mere whiff of her desire and I turn into a ravenous animal. Her taste on my tongue and her screams of pleasure are a drug I can't get enough of. I spent more time eating her out last night than actually fucking her. And if the scratches on my back are any indication, Brooke was loving every minute of it.

"How are you feeling this morning, Ace?" I grab a slice of bacon, taking a bite and trying to fight my urge to dive face first into her delicious pussy.

"A little sore but fan-fucking-tastic," she says smiling from ear to ear. "How are you feeling?"

"A little tired. My new girlfriend kept me up all night."

Brooke sits up on her elbows with a confused excited look on her face. "Girlfriend?"

"That is what I wanted to talk to you about yesterday, but you distracted me with this gorgeous fucking body," I say, running my hand along her inner thigh. "I was going to ask you if you would try giving this whole relationship stuff a go with me."

"Are you serious? I thought you didn't do relationships," she replies.

"I didn't until you showed up at my door in your bra. Looking all cute and pissed off." I chuckle taking another bite of bacon. "Look, Brooke, I haven't fallen this hard for anyone in a very long time. I feel so fucking fantastic when I'm with you. You get me like no one has before, and I just feel at home with you."

I watch the tears beginning to well up in her eyes. "I feel the same way, but I'm a little scared."

I climb up onto the table and pull her into my arms. "This scares the shit out of me too, but I want this more than anything. I want you more than anything. I know what you went through with Jake almost destroyed you, but I promise to be patient with you as long as you promise to be patient with me. I'm a little rusty at all this relationship stuff."

"I promise to be patient with you, Brian. As scared as I am about this, I'm willing to try if you are," she says, smiling softly up at me.

"Ace, you've made me the happiest man alive right now." I cup her face in my hands, kissing her tenderly. My heart is practically beating out of my chest. I've spent the last four years protecting the broken pieces of my heart and now here I am offering up what little I have left to Brooke. This is a huge gamble, but it just feels right.

Brooke looks up at me with those big blue eyes. "Can I ask you something?"

"You can ask me anything."

"What's with Ace? Believe me, I like it better than crazy bitch, but why Ace?" she asks curiously.

"That's because my luck has changed for the better since you came into my life. You're my lucky ace."

"Damn it, when did you become so sweet?" She pulls me back to her lips kissing me again.

This is all new for me too. For some reason, it just comes so easy with Brooke. I start to lean her back down to the table, ready to go for round probably eighty at this point, but she pushes me back.

"Down boy. I slaved away making you breakfast and you're going to eat it and get your strength up because we have a long day of fucking ahead of us."

"You're a real slave driver, Ace." I wink and slide down to my chair.

"Guess that means I get to whip you later when you slack off on the job." She softly giggles. "Now be a good boy and eat your breakfast, I made you a special syrup for your pancakes." She reaches behind her head and grabs the bottle of syrup. She flips open the lid and I watch in wonder as she pours the sticky liquid down along her pussy. I pull my bottom lip between my teeth when I realize she said eat my breakfast, what she really meant was eat her, and I am only too happy to oblige.

I push my plate to the side, grab Brooke by the legs, and pull her closer to the edge of the table. Her excited squeals only egg me on as I dive tongue first into her sticky wet cunt. The taste of maple syrup and Brooke drive me mad with hunger. I run my tongue over every inch of her sweet lips, sucking and licking off every last drop of syrup from her tender bud. Her hands are firmly planted in my hair, keeping me in my place. Brooke's squeals now turn to moans of pleasure as I eat out her perfect pussy.

I feel her clenching around my tongue. My dick aches to be buried deep inside her. I stand up from the table and grab Brooke, throwing her over my shoulder. She squeals in delight as I carry her back to the bedroom, then throw her onto my bed and grab a condom from my nightstand.

I slide off my boxers and go to rip open the condom, but Brooke stops me.

"Allow me," she says, a sultry grin pulling at her lips while she grabs the condom from my hand. I watch eagerly as she rips open the packet and slips the condom into her mouth. She slowly rolls the rubber down my hard length, gently sucking me as she pulls away.

"So fucking sexy," I say through gritted teeth. It takes everything I have not to ram my dick down her throat and fuck that pretty mouth of hers.

"We will put this mouth to good use later, but right now I really need to be buried deep inside that tight little pussy of yours. Now get on your fucking knees and let me see that sexy ass in the air," I demand.

She does as she's told and turns around, wiggling her gorgeous ass at me. I slam my hand down against the soft flesh of her ass, leaving my mark on her cheek. Guiding myself to her entrance, I fill her to the hilt in one giant hard thrust. We both cry out as she stretches around every inch of me. She's warm and tight and fucking dripping wet. My tongue glides up along her spine. My hand fisting into her hair, rearing her head back to expose the tender flesh of her neck. I sink my teeth into her, leaving my mark so the world fucking knows she's mine.

"You feel me inside you, Brooke?" I pull almost all the way out then slam back into her. Her hands grip the sheets, hips pushing greedily back against me, begging for more. "That's me claiming every inch of you. You are mine now, Brooke."

* * *

Tuesday morning came way too fast. The past two days with Brooke have been the best in my life. I was physically exhausted, but I felt like I could fucking fly. I was high on her and loving every minute of it.

We'd spent most of the weekend fucking in my bed, on my couch, and on top of my kitchen table. We only stopped long enough to eat, and only slept after passing out from pure exhaustion. It felt absolutely amazing to wake up with Brooke in my arms this morning. I hate having to leave her to go back to work.

"I can't believe you're leaving a beautiful naked woman in your bed to go to work." Brooke crawls across the bed to me, wrapping her arms around my body and softly kissing down my neck.

"Believe me, I'd much rather stay here with you, but duty calls," I say, reluctantly tying up the laces of my boots.

"Can't you stay for just a little bit longer?"

"You are insatiable, Brooke McCoy." I chuckle, standing up from the bed, straightening my tie.

"It's all your fault. You woke up the beast and now she's hungry for Brian." She looks up at me through her long lashes and bites her lip as her eyes devour me in my uniform.

"Well, the beast can have all she wants of me after our date tonight."

"Date? You want to take me out tonight, like on a real date?" There's that sweet sexy smile I love so much.

"We sort of went from hating each other to friends to fucking. We kind of skipped the dating phase. I will warn you now, I'm a little rusty in the dating department, so I apologize if our date is a little cheesy."

"I could go for a little cheesy. As long as I'm with you, I don't care what we do." She sits up on her knees. The sheet that was shielding her naked body is now in a pool on my bed. She slides her arms around my neck and presses her body against mine, softly kissing me. I can already feel my dick stirring in my pants. I better get out of here now before I end up throwing her on the bed and taking her again.

"I will pick you up at eight, after my shift. But now, I better go before I'm even later."

Brooke pouts and reluctantly wraps the sheet around herself and follows me out to my front door.

"Have a good day at work dear." She kisses me on the cheek then looks up at me with a smile, looking like the little wife sending her husband off to work. She's so fucking cute.

"Bye honey," I tease back, then playfully smack her ass before heading out the door.

CHAPTER SIXTEEN

Brooke

STANDING IN MY CLOSET, I sift through the racks of clothes trying to find the perfect outfit for my date with Brian. I'm feeling a mixture of nervousness and excitement. This will be the first real date I've had in years, and I'm not counting Peter, the narcissist. That night was a complete disaster, the only good thing that came from that date was me making the decision to move to Seattle. Which lead me to meeting Brian.

After Brian left for work I spent the rest of the day dancing around my apartment, unable to wipe the goofy—I'd just had the best sex of my life—grin off my face. Don't get me wrong, Jake was phenomenal in the sack, but sex with Brian is fucking mind blowing. He did things to my body I didn't think were possible. Just thinking about it is making my panties damp again.

My sexy daydreaming is brought to a halt when I hear my phone ringing from my bedroom. I walk over to my dresser and pick up it up. My mouth drops open when I see my brother Hunter's smiling face lighting up my phone.

"Holy shit, he's alive," I cheer into the phone.

"Hello, to you too, Brookie."

"Hey, I was half expecting to hear from the U.S. Embassy

that they'd found you smothered to death under a pile of hot Brazilian women."

"You got the pile of Brazilian women part right." He lets out a hardy laugh.

My brother, Hunter, is a smooth talking, tall, dark, and handsome, rich photojournalist, who could get a woman to drop her panties with just a glance from his sapphire blue eyes. His nickname all through college was the panty dropper.

"On a serious note, the reason why I've called is because I'm coming to Seattle at the end of June."

"Are fucking serious? Oh my God! I can't wait to see you," I squeal with excitement. I haven't seen my brother since I moved to Seattle nine months ago. He's been working with Travel magazine taking beautiful pictures and sleeping with women all over Europe. I've missed him like crazy. Hunter and I have been incredibly close since our mom died, we only had each other after that. My dad did the best he could for us, but he was gone a lot. Being a detective for the Boston PD kept him away from home. So Hunter stepped up and took care of me. He was the one that comforted me when I had nightmares. Took care of me when I was sick, and put too 'friendly' boyfriends in their places. He was like a second dad to me.

"I can't wait to see you, Brookie. I've missed you, Peanut."

"I've missed you, too."

"All right, before you get all misty, tell me how Seattle is treating you?" he asks changing the subject. Knowing how emotional I tend to get when we go more than a month without seeing each other.

"Seattle is treating me very well. I've made a few friends, I've started writing again and . . ." I pause taking a deep breath before mentioning Brian. "I met a guy."

"Well, that explains why you sound so happy. So who's this guy?"

I feel the butterflies beginning to flutter in my belly and I'm smiling from ear to ear. Feeling like a fucking teenager who's just been asked out by the star quarterback, I start to tell Hunter about Brian and how we didn't have the best of first meetings. Which, of course, he immediately launches into laughter when I get to the part about me showing up at Brian's door half naked. Once I get to the part about Brian being a cop, the butterflies suddenly turn into knots, and the annoying voice in my head chimes in making me question if getting involved with a cop is such a wise idea.

"Do you think I'm just setting myself up to get hurt again?" I ask with a sigh.

"Why, because Brian slept around?"

"No, because he's a cop."

"What does that have to do with anything?" he asks.

"Look what happened to Jake, and he was just an investment banker. Brian's a cop and puts himself in the line of fire every day. What if I go all in with Brian and something—"

Before I finish my sentence, Hunter interrupts me, "Brooke you're overthinking this. You never used to doubt any decision you made . . . ever. I know it's because of what happened to Jake. Look, all relationships come with risks, some are higher than others, but, when you love the person enough, you have to be willing to take that risk. From what I hear, you're crazy about this Brian guy. I haven't heard you this happy in such a long time. So my advice to you is to stop worrying about the what ifs and focus on how he makes you feel."

Hunter's right, I've never second guessed myself so much before. I've always listened to my heart and, now that Jake was gone, I was letting my head get in the way. Brian's listening to what his heart is telling him, and he's willing to hand me his heart without question. So why am I having such a hard time letting go of my own? I want to be with Brian so bad, but now it's just a matter of telling my head to shut the fuck up and let my heart do all the talking.

"I'll try, I promise. I like Brian so much I don't want to ruin it by overthinking."

"You're braver than you think, Brooke. I know you can do it. I have to go, take care and I'll call again soon. I love you Brookie."

"I love you too, Hunter."

I hang up with Hunter and take a few deep breaths. When I close my eyes, that's when Brian's crooked smile comes into view, and I feel my heart skip a beat. I focus on that smile and the warm feeling it sends through my body. I stay quiet for a moment trying to hear what my heart is trying to tell me. In my head, I can hear Brian's words saying how much he wants to be with me, and my whole body relaxes and I start to feel at peace again. Being with Brian just feels so right, now I just need to convince my head what my heart already knows.

* * *

Promptly at eight I hear a knock on the door. Brian's right on time. The butterflies begin to flutter again as I give myself one last look in the mirror. I smooth out my favorite blue strapless dress with the little pink roses, that hits me at mid-thigh, giving Brian a perfect view of my legs and easy access to little Brooke if the mood strikes him. My makeup is simple with just a touch of blush pink lip-gloss to top it off. I left my hair down in loose curls. I grab my jacket and my purse and walk across the room.

When I open the door, I'm greeted by a smiling Brian. Damn that crooked smile. I almost want to say screw the date and just pull him into my apartment and have my dirty way with him. But I stop myself knowing there will be plenty of time for that later. He's dressed in a pair of jeans and a white Henley shirt with the sleeves pulled up just below his elbows, showing off the veins in his forearms. God, I just want to run my tongue along those veins while he pounds into me.

Calm yourself Brooke.

"Wow! Ace, you look beautiful," he says eyeing me up and down with a hungry look in his eye. I can tell he's fighting the same battle I am—go out on this date or stay home and fuck.

"You're looking pretty good yourself there, handsome." I step over the threshold and gently kiss him on the cheek.

"I brought you a little something." I watch curiously as Brian moves his hand around from behind his back. "Normally the guy brings flowers, but being that you're a writer I thought you might enjoy these better." He grins, holding up a bouquet of pens and Sharpies in every color of the rainbow.

My faces lights up with joy, and I squeal with delight. "Oh my God, Brian, this is the sweetest thing anyone has ever brought me." I grab the pens from his hand, throw my arms around him, and rain kisses down all over his face.

"I take it you like it?" He chuckles.

"I absolutely love it. Now, every time I use one of these, I'll think of you. Thank you." I kiss Brian one last time then set the pens down on the side table by the door, then I close and lock the door behind me. "So where are we off to?"

Brian slides his hand into mine and we start to walk to the elevator. "I thought we'd begin the evening with dinner at The Kitchen, it's a funky little restaurant I found a few weeks ago, then take a walk down by the sound. It's beautiful at night." He pushes the down button for the elevator then turns to me. "But first, I want to do something I've been waiting to do all day." He slides his fingers under my chin, tilts me up to his lips, and tenderly kisses me. His lips are warm and soft against mine, and I can't help but to deepen our kiss. I wrap my arms around his neck pulling him tighter against me. His hands fist into my dress, and he pulls me up off my feet. Before it can go any further, the elevator dings, bringing us back to reality. We walk into the elevator, both of us breathing hard and smiling from ear to ear.

"I don't know how long I'm going to be able to go without having my dirty way with you," Brian says, giving me a sideways glance.

"Well, there's always the restaurant bathroom," I say, smiling to myself.

"You're killing me, Ace."

* * *

We manage to make it through the meal without throwing each other on the table and having each other for dinner. I'm pretty sure the other patrons are happy we fought the urge too. The food was fantastic, and the conversation was even better, which it always is with Brian. Brian filled in a few more pieces of his life, like how his birthday is on Valentine's Day. Now I have a reason to love February 14th. Fuck Valentine's Day, from now on it will be known as Brian's Day to me.

After dinner, we walk down to the waterfront. We occasionally stop for a quick make out session when no one is looking. It makes me feel like we are a couple of horny teenagers. I haven't felt this free in such a long time.

The night sky is clear and lit up with a million stars, and the sea air is softly blowing over the water. Brian and I walk hand-in-hand along the pier, stopping along the edge to watch one of the ferries coming in from the islands. It's absolutely perfect.

"This is one of my favorite spots in the city."

Brian comes up behind me, enveloping me in his strong arms. Nuzzling his face against my neck, he asks, "Why is that?"

"When I was nine, my dad brought me and my brother here to visit my aunt and uncle. It was the first vacation we took after my mom passed away. I remember the day so clearly, like it was yesterday. It was our last day here, the sun was shining and there were these massive barrages floating along the sound. My dad brought us to this exact spot and taught my brother and I how to fish. We didn't catch anything but we still had fun. It was the first time the three of us laughed. It was an amazing day."

"That sounds like a great day. Do you remember much about your mother?"

"I remember bits and pieces. She was a surgical resident at Mass General. She was studying to be a pediatric surgeon. The thing I remember most about her was her singing me to sleep every night, even if she had to work the graveyard shift, she would sing to me over the phone. She gave me my first notebook, so I could write my crazy stories down. I remember her sitting with me for hours listening to me go on and on about the intricate back stories I made up for my new toys. I feel like she is still here with me . . . watching out for me."

"That's the way I feel about my dad. Even though he is gone, I can still feel him giving me a nudge in the right direction. Like the massive nudge he gave me in the form of a beautiful blue eyed girl from Boston, who has completely captured my heart," he sweetly says, kissing the side of my cheek.

"You sweet son of a bitch. You know you are getting laid tonight, so you don't have to butter me up like this."

"I can if it's true. I know this might sound cheesy, but would you like to take a spin on the Ferris wheel?" he asks pointing to the Seattle Great Wheel all lit up in the distance.

"That's not cheesy at all. I would love to." I smile and take his hand.

We make our way through the crowd and stand in line waiting for our turn. Brian keeps his arms firmly around me, occasionally kissing my cheek. He says he's rusty with the whole dating and relationship stuff, but he's been doing an impressive job all night.

Our turn finally comes and we step into our pod and cuddle up nice and close on the bench seat. The attendant closes the doors and the ride starts to take us up. Once all the pods are filled, the Ferris wheel begins to circulate. On the second time around the ride comes to an abrupt stop and the lights go out, leaving us stuck at the very top of the ride. The attendant's voice comes over the loudspeaker and announces they're having some technical difficulties and will have it resolved as quickly as they can.

"Looks like we're going to be here for a while." Brian's hand finds its way to my knee and slowly slides up my thigh. My body begins to come to life from his touch.

"Whatever will we do to pass the time?" I ask, faking innocence.

"I think I know something we could do." A mischievous grin pulls at Brian's lips. The dark look of lust growing in his eyes tells me he wants more than just a few hot kisses. His other hand grips the back of my neck and pulls me to his lips. The hand on my leg slips further under my dress. My breath hitches when his fingers glide over the lace of my panties.

"Jesus, Ace, you're already fucking wet," he whispers against my lips. "Does this excite you, Ace? Knowing we could be caught at any moment?"

I nod my head yes. The whole night has been one long round of foreplay, so I'm already pretty amped up at this point, but the thrill of someone seeing us makes me even more excited. So much so I can feel my desire for him soaking through my dress. God damn the effect this man's having on me. Brian's lips trail down my neck.

"Such a naughty girl," he groans, nipping gently at my tender flesh. He slips his fingers into my panties, letting them sink between my wet folds. My head falls back against the glass as

Brian pushes two fingers inside me, slowly working them in and out. I can't believe I'm sitting at the top of a Ferris wheel, the world only a few feet below us, while my boyfriend is finger fucking me. I thought we'd just make out, but this, this is so much better.

"Mmm . . . Brian, I need you," I pant, my hips now riding his hand. The need to feel him buried inside me is growing ravenous.

"I want you too, Brooke, but I don't have a condom with me."

"I have an IUD and you're the first man I've slept with in two years, so I'm clean. Please baby, I need you," I plead.

He releases his fingers from me and pulls me into his lap. I quickly work open his pants and pull out his cock. He's rock hard and dripping with pre-cum. I slide my panties to the side and slowly sink down onto him. He felt good before, but now that there's nothing between us he feels fucking incredible. He's hot and hard, his skin like velvet inside me.

The moonlight illuminates Brian's face. His brown eyes sparkle in the light as they stare up at me, his soft moans turning me on even more. Brian lets out a low hiss, his head rolling back as I start to ride him. His hands grip my hips, working me harder along his length. The pod now swaying in perfect rhythm with us. Our moans echoing through the tiny space.

My lips capture his in a heated kiss, swallowing every single moan and chant of my name. I can feel him throbbing deep inside me.

"Come for me, Brian," I moan between kisses. I hold him tighter against me. His hand fisting in my hair, he pulls my lip between his teeth fighting back the deep rumbling growl emerging from his chest as he comes. Every pulse of his orgasm is sweet, sharp, and perfect, pulling me right along with him.

I press my forehead against his watching a satisfied smile stretch across his face.

"Fuck! Brooke, you're amazing." He cups my face in his hands, placing feather light kisses down along my jaw.

"You're not so bad yourself."

Just as we're feeling lost in our little bubble the lights flicker back on and the ride jerks to a start. I quickly climb off Brian's lap and straighten my dress and panties while Brian tucks himself back into his pants. We come to a stop and the attendant opens our door and we step out of our pod, smiling and holding on tightly to each other and laughing to ourselves, not caring if anyone saw what we'd just done in there. I now love Ferris wheels even more.

* * *

We make it back to our apartment building, still flying high from our adventure on the Ferris wheel. We come to a stop at my door, Brian backs me up against the door frame, looking down at me through dark hooded eyes. He leans in pressing his lips against mine, tongue sweeping in my mouth. His hands slip under my dress, fingers softly caressing my ass while his lips move down along my chest.

"Tonight was great, Brian. I had an amazing time. Thank you," I moan.

I hear a muffled, "You're welcome" come from Brian just before he dips his tongue between my breasts.

"Do you want to come in?" I ask, already knowing the answer.

"Fuck yes."

I manage to get the door open and we collapse to the floor. Brian kicks the door closed and we spend the rest of the night making love all over my apartment.

CHAPTER SEVENTEEN

Brian

I'M SITTING IN THE SQUAD car gazing out at the dark streets of Seattle. Ryder is seated next to me in the driver's seat rambling on about some chick he met at the bar. This is the first lull in the night we've had since the bars closed at two. The quiet is settling in and it's only making it more painfully obvious that I'm not at home in bed with Brooke. Thanks to a shift change, Ryder and I are stuck on the night shift for the next few weeks. It's only been a few hours but I fucking miss her already. I miss her body. I miss the way she smells; the way she tastes. I miss those gorgeous blue eyes. I especially miss being cuddled up on the couch with her watching movies. The routine we had before we started fucking hasn't changed much from when we became friends. We still have dinner and watch Netflix, except now when we get bored with what we are watching we have sex instead of falling asleep.

I've never been much of a mushy feelings kind of guy. I would always kick them to the curb once the condom hit the trash. But with Brooke, if she's not in my arms, it feels like a piece of me is missing. She makes me feel complete in a way I didn't know I needed or wanted, and now that she's not around I can feel the emptiness. I guess this is what it feels like when you fall in love. God, am I really falling in love with Brooke?

Sure, I'm crazy about her, and I can't stop thinking about her, and when I'm not with her I feel like I can't breathe, but is that love? Can you really fall in love with someone so quickly?

I was with Jillian for three years and I thought what we had was love, I thought I was happy with her. But I never felt anything like the way I do with Brooke. When I look at her, my heart literally skips a beat. I want to do everything in my power to make her as happy as she makes me.

Shit! I *am* falling in love with her.

"Hey man, I'm going to go hit the head."

"Grab me some coffee on your way back," Ryder calls out as I climb out of the cruiser.

I start walking down the street toward the coffee shop, pull my phone out of my pocket and scroll through my contacts finding Brooke's number. I know she's probably asleep, but I just need to hear her voice. It takes three rings before Brooke finally answers.

"Hi baby," Brooke answers, her sweet sleepy voice warming my heart.

"Hey Ace, did I wake you?"

"Yeah, I just fell asleep."

"I'm sorry, babe. You go back to sleep, I'll try calling you in the morning," I say, feeling slightly sorry for waking her up.

"No, it's okay. I miss your voice. How's the night shift going?"

"It fucking sucks because it's keeping me from my girl."

"I love it when you call me your girl." I can almost hear the smile on her face through the phone.

"So how is my girl doing? Get any more writing done? I loved the new pages you sent me." I really must be falling for this girl. She's got me reading again, to the point that I'm becoming obsessed with her words.

"Really? You really liked it?" she asks with a yawn.

"Granted, I know nothing about the genre that you write, but I think the hard-on it gave me must mean it's good."

She giggles into the phone. "Then I did my job right. Did you find the little gift I left you on your keychain?" she asks. I have no clue what gift she is talking about. Curious I reach into my pocket and pull out my keys. I examine the ring carefully, that's when I see it, a small silver key with the initial B etched in the silver.

"Brooke is this what I think it is?" Did she really give me a key to her place?

"If it's a key to my apartment, then yes it is." The sleepy tone in her voice turns to excitement. "In case I happen to fall asleep again before you get home from your shift you can use the key to let yourself in. I know I'm not going to be able to go weeks without you holding me while we sleep. This way you can come and go when you please and we can still see each other a little before you go to work."

I hold the key between my fingers and stare at it. She gave me a key to her apartment. An actual key giving me an all access pass to my girl. This is a huge step for the both of us and it feels right. I've practically been living at her place since we started dating. This amazing woman has me completely pussy whipped and I'm loving every minute of it. "To think I was going to just break down your door to get to you, but this is a better idea." We both laugh. "This is really sweet of you, Ace, thank you. I miss you already, so I will be using this key later."

"I miss you too Brian. It wasn't the same watching The Walking Dead without you tonight."

"You watched it without me?"

"I only made it through half an episode before I turned it off. It didn't feel right watching it without you. Especially, since I couldn't hide my face in your chest when the scary parts came on." She lets out a sad sigh.

"I like that part, usually ends with us making out on your couch," I say, trying to get her to laugh.

"That's not the only thing it leads to," she says in a yawn mixed with a giggle.

"If that couch could talk. Ace you sound tired. You go back to bed and I will see you in the morning."

"Okay. Goodnight Brian and stay safe." She yawns again.

"I will. Goodnight Ace." I push end on the call and stuff my phone back into my pocket. My steps become lighter as I walk to the coffee shop. I am definitely falling for this woman.

⋆ ⋆ ⋆

I push the key into the deadbolt, turning it until I hear the click of the lock. Brooke's apartment is dark and quiet when I step inside. I drop my duffle bag and my jacket by the door and work off my boots before walking to Brooke's bedroom. Brooke is sleeping peacefully with the blanket pulled down enough that I can see that she is wearing my Seattle PD t-shirt. I'm actually slightly jealous that my shirt has been on top of her all night instead of me. Stripping down to my boxers, I climb into bed next to her. My arms snake around her, pulling her to me. She lets out a soft moan as our bodies come together. I'm instantly at peace.

"You used your key," she says.

"I couldn't go a minute longer without you in my arms," I reply, placing a soft kiss against her neck.

Brooke wiggles out of my arms to sit up and pull off my shirt. She tosses it to the floor then lays back down next to me. We are skin to skin and my dick stirs to life. Doesn't help that she's gently rubbing her ass against my crotch. I need to be inside her. I work my boxers off my hips and kick them the rest of the way off. I lift her leg up over my hip. My pelvis thrusting against her. My dick pushing between her legs, but not inside, and it has me hard and throbbing with need. I slide a hand up her stomach to cover her breast and palm her hardened peak.

Her hand reaches behind my head, guiding my lips back to her neck. I kiss and lick her there. "Brian, please," she begs. I grip my length and guide my thick tip to her entrance. I thrust inside her filling her to the hilt. Our bodies rock together as we make love until the sun comes up.

CHAPTER EIGHTEEN

Brooke

"HERE YOU GO SWEET LOLA." I bend down placing Lola's food dish in front her and give her a rub behind the ears. With Brian working the night shift, I offered to help take care of Lola while he's away at work. It's kind of nice having her here to keep me company while Brian sleeps. We go on runs together and she sleeps at my feet while I write at my desk. She's my little buddy.

I straighten and pick up my coffee mug from the kitchen table. I take the last few sips of the dark roasted goodness. Coffee has become my best friend over the past couple weeks. My whole sleeping schedule is completely off since I gave Brian access to my apartment. Giving him a key to my place was the best thing I ever did. It just seemed like the logical thing to do. This way, we still get to have a few hours of sleep together before I had to be up for the day. I love getting woken up with either Brian's dick in me or his tongue, then he spends the rest of the morning holding me in his arms while he sleeps. One of the things I do miss is being able to sit over dinner and talk with him, which is why tonight I have decided to surprise Brian with dinner at the precinct.

I managed to wrangle Ryder into helping me by bribing him

with food—he's so easy. He messaged me a half an hour ago letting me know they'd be heading back to the precinct around ten to finish up their reports for the week and take a dinner break before heading out for checkpoint duty. Which is the perfect amount of time for me to bring Brian a special picnic dinner.

I set my empty mug in the sink then fill Lola's water dish. I finish wrapping up the meatloaf sandwiches, homemade potato chips, and Brian's favorite bacon maple donuts. I pack everything up in my picnic basket, tossing in a couple bottles of water and some napkins. I give Lola one last pat goodbye then head out to the precinct.

Arriving at the station promptly at ten, I quickly message Ryder of my arrival then head inside to wait for him to escort me to their work station. The precinct is quiet and almost empty, except for a few ladies working dispatch and two officers working the front desk, all give me a curious once over before returning their attention to the computer screens in front of them. A few minutes later Ryder comes through the double doors and escorts me down the hallway and through the row of empty desks to where Brian is sitting working on the week's reports.

"Look who I found wandering around out front," he announces as we walk up to Brian's desk.

Brian looks up, his hardened expression fading to a soft smile when he sees me. "Ace, what are you doing here?" He stands up from his chair and pulls me into his arms, spins me around before setting me back down on my feet.

"I missed you and thought I'd surprise you with dinner." I set the basket down on the desk and reach inside to grab one of the sandwiches, handing it to Ryder as payment for his help. I couldn't help but giggle as he brought it up to his nose taking a big deep inhale and making gargling noises like Homer from

The Simpsons.

"I'm going to go eat this in the break room and leave you two love birds alone." He turns and starts to walk away.

"Enjoy your dinner, and thank you again, Ryder," I call out to him.

"Anytime Brooke. Especially if you pay me in food," he calls back, waving his sandwich in the air.

As soon as Ryder is gone, Brian slides his fingers under my chin, tilting my head up and places a soft kiss on my lips. *Damn, I've missed those lips.*

"This is a pleasant surprise." He grins. "So what did you bring me?" he asks eyeing the basket sitting on his desk.

"I made meatloaf sandwiches, homemade potato chips, and your favorite, maple bacon donuts." I hand Brian a sandwich as he takes his seat again. Pushing his paperwork aside, I sit up on his desk, letting my purple wrap dress fall open just enough to show off my long, lean legs.

"Damn woman, you spoil me." He flashes me that gorgeous sexy crooked smile, licking his lips while his eyes trail up my legs.

I watch as Brian takes a big bite of his sandwich, letting out a loud satisfied moan while he chews. "Damn this is good," he mumbles, taking another big bite.

"I'm glad you like it." I pop a chip in my mouth and look over the mess of paperwork and empty coffee cups on Brian's desk. My scanning stops on a book with Detective Practice Exam printed on the spine. I reach across the messy desk and pull it out from under the pile of papers and hold it up. "Brian are you thinking about becoming a detective?"

"Oh yeah. I've thought about it. But I don't think I'm going to take the test." He grabs the book from my hand and opens one of his drawers, stuffing it inside.

"Why not?" I ask.

"I don't really want to talk about it." He brushes me off and takes another bite of his sandwich.

Since meeting Brian, this is the first time I've seen him shy away from anything. He's always been straightforward with me, and he is the type that if he wanted something he does everything in his power to get. Me, being a prime example of that.

I set my bag of chips down and climb into Brian's lap straddling his waist. I cup his chin bringing his eyes back to mine and that's when I see what he's trying to hide. I can see the wavering confidence in his eyes. The broken man that has for so many years been told by the woman who was supposed to love and support him that he wasn't good enough. I swear, if I ever see this Jillian bitch on the street, I'll run her over with my car. The way she used and manipulated Brian makes me sick to my stomach. You're supposed to help the ones you love reach their dreams. Not tear them down to build yourself up.

In this moment, I see Brian for all of him. Behind the cocky attitude and charm, I see his pain, his fear. He's broken and bruised, and I know without hesitation that I can put the broken pieces of this man back together and show him how good love can really be.

"Don't shut me out, Brian. Why don't you want to take the test?"

"Because I know I'm not good enough," he says turning away from me again.

I pull him back to me. "Is this because of Jillian? No, I know it's because of her. Brian, you can't let her words, her insecurities, keep you from following your dreams."

"What if she's right?"

"Fuck her. You are Brian-fucking-Gamble, and you are the best damn cop the Seattle PD has. If you want to be a fucking detective then damn it, you go for it. I know you don't believe in yourself right now, but I do. I believe in you with every ounce of my being. I know without a shadow of a doubt that you'll make the best damn detective, and I'll do everything in my power to have you believe in yourself again." I flash him a reassuring smile.

"Really?" he asks curiously.

"Hell, yes. I'll help you study. Give you quizzes. I'll be your very own cheerleading squad," I say with a proud smile.

I see a smirk beginning to tug at the corner of his mouth. "Just to see you in a cheerleading uniform would be worth it." He wiggles his eyebrows at me. And there is the Brian I fell for. "All right, I'll take the test. You're quite persuasive, Ace. Why are you so good to me?"

"Because I love you." As soon as the words leave my lips my hands slam down over my mouth. I sit there wide-eyed as my words hang in the air. I can't believe that just slipped out. I knew I was falling hard for Brian, but I hadn't even admitted to myself that I was in love with him, let alone ready to admit it to him. Maybe this is my heart finally taking control and doing what my head is too scared to do.

"Brooke, did you just say you loved me?" The initial shock begins to fade from his face as he waits for my reply.

All I could do was nod, yes. Yes. *Yes, I fucking love this man.* He's completely turned my world upside down, brought me back to life and I love him.

"Did you mean it?" he asks, pulling my hands away from my mouth.

"Yes," I say, more confidently this time.

"Good, because I love you too, Brooke."

I feel the tears beginning to stream down my face. "You do?"

"Hell yes." He smiles from ear to ear. "I'm fucking crazy about you, Brooke." He reaches his hand up, wiping my tears with his thumb.

"Say it again," I demand, needing to hear his words again.

"I love you, Brooke McCoy."

I cup his face in my hands, pulling him to my lips.

"I . . . Love . . . You . . . Brian," I say between each kiss.

"I wish I wasn't at work because I really need to make love to the woman I love right now."

"I have an idea." I climb off of Brian's lap and grab his hand leading us over to the only office with a door, the Captain's office. We step inside and I lock the door and close the blinds to give us some privacy.

"You're a bad, bad girl, Ace." Brian presses me against the door, the metal blinds covering the window digging into my back. "First the Ferris wheel and now in my precinct. You're full of surprises." He reaches a hand between us, pulling open the bow holding my dress closed. His eyes darken as my dress falls open, exposing the pink lace bra and thong I was wearing the night we met.

"Did you have this all planned?" he growls.

"Yes." Our lips finally meet, tongues fighting for dominance in my mouth, and our kiss hot, hard, and full of need. I pull him tighter against me. My body is aching to feel the weight of him on top of me.

I reach up and remove his tie and my hands make quick work at unbuttoning his shirt. As good as he looks in his uniform, and no matter how much I want him to fuck me while still dressed in it, my need to see him out of it has won. I yank it from his pants and slide it off his shoulders. He pulls his undershirt over his head, tossing it on the couch behind him. I run my hands down his chest, tracing the planes of his stomach. I love his body, every curve of his muscular frame is perfection. I slowly walk around him, hands exploring every inch of his beautiful back. I kiss and lick down the line of his spine and place a feather light kiss just above his ass.

Slowly, I walk back around to face him then drop to my knees, wickedly grinning up at him when I see his erection already straining against his pants. I lightly brush my hand against him, eliciting a jagged hiss. Slowly, I untie and removed his boots. I work open his belt and unbutton his pants, sliding them and his boxers off his hips in one motion. His erection springs free already dripping with cum.

I start off slow, licking and sucking on his balls, knowing how much he loves it. Flattening my tongue, I slowly lick up his shaft, savoring how good he tastes. The veins pulse against my tongue. His deep moans fill the air as I flick my tongue around his tip, lapping up his salty sweetness.

"God damn, this is so fucking hot," he growls, gathering my hair in his hand to get a better view.

I take him into my mouth inch by delicious inch. I love the way he feels and the way he tastes. I wrap a hand around his thick length, squeezing and stroking in rhythm with my mouth.

My teeth gently graze and my tongue swirls around his impressive thick length. He has a fierce dark look in his eyes as he gazes down at me, and it sends a jolt that hits me right in my pussy making it grow heavy with need.

Next thing I know Brian's pulling me up off the floor and carrying me over to the desk, clearing its contents off in one fast sweep of his arm. He spins me around and roughly bends me over the desk. The cold wood feels good against my hot skin. He presses his hot hard body against mine and I can feel his rock hard cock pressing against my ass. I can't help but to grind my hips against his length, evoking a deep growl from his chest.

"I've dreamt of what you'd look like in these." His low dark tone making my whole body shudder. His fingers follow the lace along my inner thigh to between my legs and ghosting along my slit through my thong.

He hooks the delicate lace, rips it clean from my body, and tosses the tattered remains to the floor. As he runs his rough hands down along my ass before giving it a nice hard slap, it causes me to jump and makes my body spring to life.

"Mmm harder," I command.

He leans over me again and whispers in my ear, "Does my sweet little Ace like it rough?" His dark tone sending a chill down my spine.

"Fuck yes," I softly moan, needing more.

"Such a dirty girl. My dirty girl." His hand strikes me again, this time hard enough to leave a print on my ass. It takes everything I have to fight back my screams of pleasure as he strikes me again and again.

Brian drops to his knees and places feather light kisses over my reddened flesh then sinks his teeth into my tender skin, forcing me to cry out in pleasure filled pain. Fuck! I like this side of my Brian.

He grabs two handfuls of my ass and spreads me open. I have to brace my hands on the edge of the desk to keep myself steady when I feel the tip of his tongue plunge inside my wet channel.

He flattens his tongue taking long slow teasing licks from my clit up to my ass, circling my tight little hole. "I miss tasting your sweet fucking pussy," he groans, pushing his tongue back inside me.

"Oh God, Brian, that feels so fucking good," I cry out.

"Mmm." I can feel his moans vibrate against me. His hand cracks across my right ass cheek, making every muscle in my nether regions clench around his nimble tongue. He's eating me out like a starved man. With one last flick of his tongue, the waves of pleasure come crashing over me as I come all over his mouth.

Brian slows his pace and laps up every last drop of me. He

stands back up and flips me over onto my back, he wraps my legs around his waist, and before I have a chance to catch my breath, he rams into me, forcing me up the desk.

"Fuck! Brooke, you're so tight," he growls as he starts working himself in and out of my slick cunt.

I pull him down to my lips kissing him deep and hard. My nails digging into his back as he pounds harder and harder into me. The desk creaking and squeaking under us.

Brian pulls me up into his arms, keeping his lips locked on mine as he pulls me up from the desk and sits back on the couch behind us. I reach behind me unhooking my bra and tossing it to the floor. He presses his face between my breasts, sucking and leaving little red marks in his wake. His warm mouth feels so good, I can't get enough of it.

We find the rhythm of our own sultry dance, one we are becoming all too familiar with. My hips grind around and around as he thrusts up to meet me, and his hands dance along my body, gripping my hips, working me harder along his cock and hitting me in my, oh so sweet, spot.

"Fuck, you feel so good," I moan, trying to keep quiet, but finding it harder and harder as I get closer to the edge.

"That's it Ace, come all over my cock."

Brian pulls me to his lips swallowing my moans and screams, driving harder into me. My body shakes as waves of pleasure wash over me again and again. Brian's thrusts become more erratic and wild as he works himself to the brink, cock throbbing and pulsing as he fills me with every last drop of him.

I fall against his chest, listening as his breathing calms. His hands gently trail up and down my back. I'm in heaven with the man I love.

CHAPTER NINETEEN

Brian

BROOKE AND I SIT IN silence just holding each other. Kissing and touching as much as we can before reality hits us and I have to go back to work. I don't want this to fucking end. I want to take her home and lie with her in my arms for the rest of the night. This woman loves me, and I love her. This all feels like a dream and, if I let her go, I'm afraid I will wake up and she'll be gone.

But sadly, our quiet moment is interrupted by a knocking on the door.

"Hey Brooke, if you are done with my partner, I kind of need him back. We have checkpoint duty in less than twenty minutes."

"Way to kill the mood, Ryder," I call out.

Brooke and I both laugh. "I don't want you to go. I just want to kiss you all night while you hold me in your arms," Brooke pouts, sticking her lip out at me.

"I don't want to go either, but in just a few short hours I will be crawling into bed with you and you can kiss me all you want."

"That sounds like heaven." She smiles, then climbs off my lap.

We dress in silence unable to take our eyes off each other. I finish straightening my tie and watch as Brooke grabs the remains of her panties from the floor. She glides over to me and stuffs the tattered remnants in my uniform pocket and flashes me a sexy triumphant smile.

"A little memento of our fun tonight. And now every time you come in here you won't be thinking about how the Captain is going to suspend your ass. Instead, you'll be thinking how you fucked the woman you love all over his pristine office." She tenderly kisses me one last time. "Now, go keep the streets of Seattle safe, Officer Gamble."

She starts to walk toward the door then turns back. "I love you, Brian."

"I love you too, Brooke."

Her face lights up at my words and she blows me a kiss before opening the door and steps back out into the precinct.

God, I fucking love this woman.

Walking over to the door, I lean up against the frame and watch her hips sway as she gets further and further away, until she finally disappears through the double doors. Out of the corner of my eye I see Ryder slide up next to me. He peaks inside the office and examines the destruction.

"The Captain's office," he sighs, dropping his shaking head. "My game is slipping."

"Your game is fine asshole. If I remember correctly, you and Julie from dispatch fucked on the hood of his car."

"I almost forgot about that. He still to this day doesn't know whose ass prints were all over his precious black Lexus." He laughs to himself. "Now that you got that out of your system, let's go fuck with some drunk college idiots."

CHAPTER TWENTY

Brooke

I PACE BACK AND FORTH in my living room, stopping occasionally to look out the peep hole of my door to check if Brian is walking out of the elevator yet. I haven't slept a wink since I got home from the precinct. The adrenaline from telling Brian I loved him is still pumping through my veins. My big mouth finally did some good for once.

I do love him and he loves me. Just hearing his voice in my head repeating it back to me makes my heart soar. If someone had asked me three months ago if I thought I'd ever find love again, I would have told them hell no. I'd had the great love of my life and he was now gone. But meeting Brian and spending so much time with him, I'm rethinking my old-fashioned way of thinking.

I hear the ding of the elevator, and I run over to my door checking the peephole for Brian, who's exiting the elevator. I fumble with the locks in my haste to get to him. I unlatch the deadbolt and run out the door with Lola right on my heels. Brian drops his duffle bag on the floor and holds his arms out for me. Jumping into his arms, I wrap myself around him and rain down kisses all over his face while Lola barks excitedly and jumps up on her hind legs.

"I see my girls are happy to see me." He chuckles.

"Welcome home, baby."

"This is best welcome home I've ever gotten."

I jump down to let Brian kneel down to give Lola a few rubs behind the ears. She follows suit licking all over Brian's face.

Brian picks up his duffle bag and we walk back to my apartment. "So how are my two favorite girls doing?"

"Good. We've been missing you, though."

"I've missed you both too. Especially you." He drops his bag at my door then slides his hand around the back of my neck pulling me to his lips and gently kisses me. "Still love me?" he asks.

"Yes, I still love you, Brian," I say, giving him a reassuring smile.

"Did you hear that, Lola? This beautiful woman says she loves me." He looks down at Lola, who lets out an approving bark. "Yes, I love her too." He flashes me a tired grin.

"Baby, you look exhausted. Why don't you come inside and get some sleep," I suggest.

"I think I'm going to crash at my place for a bit. I know if I step foot in your apartment I won't be able to keep myself from ravaging you, and I really need to get some sleep."

I feel slightly bad for not making him sleep instead of fucking me and it didn't help that I would also wake him up in the afternoons for a quickie. "You go get some sleep, and me and Lola will see you before you go to work."

"Before I go I want to ask you something. I have some vacation days coming up after my shift change and I wanted to see if you would like to come with me to my cabin on Orcas Island."

"You have a cabin on the islands?" I ask.

"It's just a small place by the water. I thought we could get away from all the distractions of work for a few days. How does that sound?"

"That sounds absolutely amazing and I can't wait."

"Good, now come here and give me a kiss goodnight."

⋆ ⋆ ⋆

I spend most of the morning finishing up the rough draft of my book. The book that Brian has inspired. I am so proud with how this one has turned out. It's a sweet second chance story and much lighter reading than the heavier stuff I've written before. Probably because I'm in a much happier place in my life. Either way, my editor and publisher love the book and want me to turn it into a series. Finally, everything in my life is coming together.

Sitting in the middle of my bedroom floor, I pull the tape off the last and final box from my big move. I've been living in this apartment for six months, taking my dear sweet time making it my home. This is the first time I've had my own place, and it's taken me a while to find my own style. When I had roommates back in New York, our place was a mish mash of hand me down furniture and found items on the street, then when I moved in with Jake, his place was already fully furnished in his taste. It never really felt like my home. This place is mine. My little home where I can have all my books around me and my favorite little knick-knacks I've collected over the years. But, to be honest, I was being a tad bit lazy. Unpacking sucks.

I pull out picture frames filled with old photos of my brother and me, and my dad in Boston. Those were some of the happiest and worst times of my life. After my mom died, my dad moved us to a duplex right next to my grandmother in Charlestown, which was just across the bridge from Boston. My mother's medical expenses ate up all of our savings. My dad had to sell our house in Dorchester to pay off the rest.

It wasn't an easy move in the beginning. My brother and

I were uprooted from the only home we'd ever known to a neighborhood that wasn't quite so warm and welcoming to a cop moving in on their territory. Our house was egged countless times and my dad received death threats at least once a week. But when you move to an area that has more armored truck robbers than most of Boston, it was to be expected.

My grandmother wasn't exactly the easiest to get along with either. She was a tough old broad. I know she was just trying to keep my brother and me from slipping down the same road most of the kids that grew up in our neighborhood did, but man, could her words cut you like a fucking knife. I busted my ass in school so I could get a scholarship and move my ass the hell out of there.

I do miss the times with my dad. He might have been gone a lot with work, but he always made sure he gave us his undivided attention when he was home and made every moment count. He would take us to Red Sox games in the summer and we'd freeze our asses off at Patriot games in the winter. He'd take us camping and fishing. But my favorite times with him were when it was just him and me sitting on the couch, and I would read him the latest epic princess tale I'd written. I'm sure he would've rather been watching the game, but he sat through every minute of it with a big smile on his face. I miss that. I miss him.

All my father's hard work in Boston paid off in the form of a job in the special crimes unit with the FBI in D.C. His ultimate dream job. The job keeps him even busier than when he was a detective, so I see him even less now. It sucks, but at least I still have Hunter, who calls me between bed hops.

I set the pictures down and pull out a layer of bubble wrap and a glimmer of silver catches my eye. My heart stops when I realize it's Jake's ashes. I reach into the box and pull out the silver urn. One of his last wishes in his will was for me to spread his ashes around the coffee shop where we first met, the spot in Central Park where he first told me he loved me, and over the Brooklyn Bridge where he proposed. But I was never able to bring myself to do it because I was too selfish and didn't want to lose the last bit of him I had left. Now, here he is with me in Seattle. It's true, you can't run from your past.

I could travel to the ends of the earth and Jake's memory would still find me. The guilt that plagues me about moving on is because I never truly said goodbye to Jake before he passed away. By the time I made it to the hospital, he was already gone.

I get up from the floor taking Jake with me. Grabbing my bag and placing the urn inside, I slip on my shoes. I grab my jacket from the hook by the door and head out to the elevator. I need to see Lucy. I need to hear her say it's okay for me to let Jake go.

I step out into the cool spring afternoon where the gray clouds are heavy in the sky and the smell of looming rain fills the air. I quicken my pace when I start to feel the tears welling up in my eyes. The reality of saying goodbye to the first man I've ever loved hits me like a ton of bricks. My fast walk turns into a sprint as I turn the corner and see Lucy's shop. Flinging open the door, I frantically step inside. Lucky's sitting on the counter flipping through a US Weekly magazine and blowing bubbles with her gum. There are a couple people sipping coffee in the back corner and Lucy is nowhere to be found.

Lucky looks up from her magazine. "Hey, girly." Her smile quickly fades to concern when she sees my red tear-stained eyes.

"Where's Lucy? Lucy," I call out. Trying into keep it calm, but I'm failing miserably.

Lucky jumps off the counter and walks over to me. "Lucy's on the phone with her coffee distributor. What's going on honey? Here, sit down." She helps me to one of the empty tables at the front of the shop. Her face is turning to a mixture of worry and terror when the ugly crying kicks in. She hands me a napkin for my tears. "Did Brian break up with you? Did that asshole do this?" she asks trying her best to be a supportive friend.

"No, it's not Brian," I squeak out between sobs.

"I'm sorry Brooke, I don't really know how to handle all this. I'm just a dead-behind-the-eyes stripper." The panic now growing in her eyes.

"Just get me, Lucy. Get Lucy now!" I demand.

"Okay. Okay. Get Lucy," she mumbles then runs back to the kitchen, stumbling over a table as she bolts for the door.

I sit quietly sobbing. I've spent two years building an emotional wall around the memories of Jake, keeping them safe and keeping me from having to actually deal with losing him. Now that wall is crumbling down, and I feel like I'm drowning.

Lucy comes running out of the kitchen with Lucky trailing close behind her. She arrives at my table with a box of Kleenex in hand and takes a seat next to me. "I'm here, sweetie. What's going on?" She hands me a tissue then sweeps my hair behind my ear.

I suck in a few quick breaths. "Brian . . ." I suck in another haggard breath. "I told Brian I loved him." I sob. "And . . . and he said it back."

"Oh honey, this is good news. Why are you crying?" She pulls another tissue from the box and starts helping to wipe my tears away.

"Well, I know that would make me cry. Well, no, more like run screaming for the hills," Lucky chimes in, taking a seat across the table. Lucy flashes her a

disapproving glare.

"My tears are because of this." I reach into my bag and pull out Jake's urn and set on the table. The three of us stare at the elephant in the room.

Lucky's head cocks to the side as she examines it. "What the hell is that?"

"It's Jake," I reply.

"I thought he'd be taller," she says nonchalantly.

"Okay, you need to go away," Lucy scolds.

"What did I say?"

"Just go make yourself useful and get Brooke one of everything from the pastry case," she orders.

"Okay fine. Brooke, I'm gonna hook you up, girl." Lucky gets up from the table, walks over to the coffee bar, and sets to work pulling out desserts from the pastry case.

"Okay, so you told Brian you loved him then found Jake's ashes, so then what happened?" she asks calmly.

"I started to realize the reason why I had been having such a hard time with moving on before I met Brian is because I never really let Jake go, and now I want to truly say goodbye to him and it's breaking my heart." The tears start streaming down even harder. Feelings suck!

"Brooke, honey." Lucy pulls me into her arms. "No wonder you're a mess."

A mess is putting it mildly. I'm a fucking basket case. I finally find someone who makes me ecstatically happy and here I am still holding onto my first love.

Lucky comes back to the table with a tray filled with cupcakes, cookies, and scones. The couple that was sitting in the back come walking toward us, staring at me while I sob all over Lucy.

"What? Haven't you ever seen a woman crying?" Lucky barks as the couple quickly passes by our table. "Yeah, you better keep walking," she threatens as they bolt out the door.

Lucy lets out a frustrated sigh at Lucky then turns her attention back to me. Gently stroking my hair she asks, "Do you really love Brian?"

"With all my heart," I mumble into her shoulder.

"Then sweetie, you need to put your big girl panties on and do what you should've done two years ago . . . let Jake go. I know it's hard, believe me, I know. Saying goodbye to Colton was the toughest thing I've ever had to do, but it's the only thing that's going to help you to move on."

I sit up, grab another tissue, and wipe away my tears, and feel relieved knowing that Lucy felt the same way when she lost Colton. "Your right, Lucy. It's time for me to say goodbye. Will you guys come with me to spread Jake's ashes?"

"Of course, we will." Lucy warmly smiles.

"We will?" Lucky groans, taking a bite from a large chocolate chip cookie.

Lucy reaches over and slaps Lucky on the arm. "Yes . . . we will," she repeats herself, narrowing her eyes at Lucky.

⋆ ⋆ ⋆

A half an hour later, we find ourselves wandering down the green belt, along Elliot Bay, trying to find the perfect spot to spread Jake's ashes. Once we pass by Myrtle Park, I spot an ideal little secluded strip of beach. I leave Lucky and Lucy up on the trail. I need to do this on my own, but I also need to know someone's going to be there for me when I'm finished.

I carefully walk over the rocky beach to an old weathered log on the edge of the water and take a seat. I pull out Jake's urn from my bag and stare at it for a few minutes before I look up and out across the water. The gray clouds are rolling in the distance, and the only sound is the waves crashing against the rocks.

"Hi Jakey." I close my eyes, taking in a deep calming breath, "I know you're probably riding around in your old beat up truck with your brother right about now, but I really need to talk to you. I'm kind of losing it because I've been a bit selfish. I've locked you away so I wouldn't have to say goodbye. But I've met someone, and I'm falling pretty hard for him. I've actually fallen in love with him." The tears begin to fall from my eyes again. "I think you'd like him. Like you, he had me pegged the moment we met, and he too knows how to push my buttons." I let out a little chuckle. "He makes me so damn happy, and I want to make it work with him. In order for me to do that, I have to let you go." I suck in a sharp breath. This goodbye feels like a jagged knife slowly being pulled out of my heart. "You were my best friend. The love of my life. You took a broken girl and made her believe in herself and in happy endings. And for that, I will always love you. But now I have to let you go. And I need to know you're okay with me moving on. I just need some sort of sign."

Just as I finish speaking, the sun breaks through the dark clouds shining a beautiful ray of golden light across the bay, and I know it's Jake telling me he's okay with letting me go. A relieved smile pulls at my lips. "Thank you."

I pull open the lid of the urn and lift up a handful of ashes. "Goodbye, Jake. You'll always have a place in my heart. I love you." I sprinkle them over the rocks. As the last of the ashes fall from my hand, Lucy and Lucky join me on the log, wrapping their arms around me.

"Feeling better?" Lucky asks.

"Much better. Thank you both for coming here with me." I rest my head on Lucy's shoulder. I seriously wouldn't know what I'd do without these two amazing women in my life. Probably go slightly mad. They are more than friends, they are my sisters.

"Of course, sweetheart. I know you feel like you're going

through this alone, but we will always be here for you." Lucy kisses the top of my head and rubs my shoulder. "You've become a wonderful friend and sister to Lucky and to me. Men will always come along, but what the three of us have is eternal. We are your family now, Brooke."

CHAPTER TWENTY-ONE

Brian

YOU'RE A PATHETIC WASTE OF space, and one day your lovely new girlfriend will open her eyes and see it too. You're a loser Brian, and you destroy everything you touch. Loser . . . loser.

I jump up from the bed, another damn nightmare tearing me away from my sleep. Jillian's words still ring in my ears. I haven't had a dream like that since I started seeing Brooke. Of course, Jillian *would* start haunting me now that I've actually found someone that cares about me. I can't let her words get to me. Brooke's the best thing to happen to me, and I'm not going to fuck it up.

I pull the covers back and rest my feet on the floor, running my hands through my messy hair. I reach over to my nightstand and pick up my phone to check the time. As soon as I pick it up it starts to ring. Looking at the screen, I see Lucy's number. Odd, she rarely ever calls me.

"Hey Lucy, is something wrong?" I ask.

"It's Brooke, she found Jake's ashes today while she was unpacking some boxes and she had a mild breakdown. And before you freak out, she's fine now. But she needs you," she replies.

Without hesitation, I bolt up from my bed and run to my closet to grab some clothes. "Where are you guys?"

"We're at a little beach about a quarter of a mile from the Olympic Sculpture Garden."

"Okay, I'm on my way."

I hang up with Lucy, frantically get dressed, and lace up my boots. My mind is racing wondering what's going on with Brooke. I grab my jacket as I run out the door. I anxiously tap my foot against the tile floor of the elevator as it descends down to the garage.

I jump on my motorcycle and speed the whole way, weaving through traffic. I just have to get to my girl, she's hurting and needs me. I park my bike and run down the greenbelt looking for Lucy. She waves me down when she spots me.

"Lucy what's going on? Where's Brooke?" I say, as the panic rips through me.

"Calm down, Brian. She's fine, she just had to say her final goodbyes to Jake. Lucky and I have done everything we can to make her feel better, but what she really needs is you." She places a calming hand on my shoulder.

"I don't even know what to say to her." I've never gone through anything close to what Brooke did with Jake. I have no clue as to what to say or do to comfort her in this situation.

"She doesn't need your words. She just needs you to be here for her. To hold her and let her cry on your shoulder. That will mean more than words." She pats my shoulder and gives me a reassuring smile before leaving with Lucky.

Okay, I can do this. My girl needs me and I'm going to be here for her. I walk across the rocks to where Brooke is standing by the water. "Brooke," I quietly say, not wanting to startle her. She turns around and gives me a small smile.

"Brian, what are you doing here?" she asks. I can see her red tear-stained eyes brighten up as I step closer.

"Lucy called me," I reply, inching closer.

"Of course she did. Brian, there's something we need to talk about." Her voice turns to a more serious tone and it makes me slightly nervous. Maybe along with saying goodbye to Jake she's also realized she could do better than me.

"Brooke, can we talk about this at home, it's starting to rain." I feel the raindrops hitting the top of my head.

"No, I need to say this before I talk myself out of it." My heart leaps into my throat. "Before, I used to think that we only have one great love in our lives, and, for the longest time, I believed I had mine with Jake. After he died I thought that was it, so I stopped looking, because, who hits the jackpot twice in their life?"

"Brooke, I know you have this weird delusion about love but have you ever stopped to think that you might be the great love of my life?" This woman is the best thing to happen in my life and I'm not going to let this crazy delusion of hers keep us from being together. I love her too damn much to go down without a fight.

"Yes, and if you'll shut your mouth and let me finish professing my love for you, we can go home," she snaps at me.

I put my hands up in surrender and shut my mouth.

"I used to think that *until* I met you. It took me a long time to figure out why fate brought me to Seattle. Why it took me six months to find the perfect apartment and, I realize now, it's because it was leading me to you. I will always love Jake—"

"I would never expect anything less. He was a big part of your life," I say interrupting her again.

"Brian, please let me finish."

"Okay, I'm sorry, again."

"I will always love him, but I realize now that he was brought into my life to prepare me to love you. When I met Jake, I was in an awful place in my life, kind of like you were when we met. He showed me how to love and to believe in myself. To believe that I deserved to have a happy ending. You're my happy ending Brian. I know it's crazy, because we haven't known each other that long, but I can feel it in my bones that we're supposed to be together. I'm all in. As crazy as all of this is, I am in this with you for better or for worse." A smile erupts across her face.

That is all I needed to hear. I close the gap between us and scoop Brooke into my arms, kissing her as the rain begins to pour down on us. This beautiful woman came into my life like a spring rain washing away my past. She's starting to make me believe I deserve her and, that I, too, deserve to be happy for once in my life. Brooke is my home now. She is . . . the love of my life.

CHAPTER TWENTY-TWO

Brooke

FRIDAY IS FINALLY HERE AND my excitement had me up at dawn, showered, and packed, before the sun had even fully entered the sky. I welcomed Brian home from his shift with a smile and a, God-I'm-so-happy-to-see-you blowjob, before he went to bed to sleep before we leave for his cabin.

To keep myself from sitting at home watching the minutes tick by on the clock, I went and helped Lucy with the morning rush at her coffee shop. Afterward, we grabbed a bite to eat and consumed one too many margaritas.

Tipsy and not ready to go home yet—Brian's still asleep and Lucy's daughter is visiting her grandparents for the weekend—Lucy and I decide to head to the pottery class Lucky's teaching down at a small art studio in West Seattle. We put on our aprons and each take a seat at the two empty pottery wheels in the back of the class. We're sitting next to a couple of guys who look like they've just stepped out of an L.L. Bean catalog and are desperate to pick up women attending the class.

Lucky finally walks into the room looking very much the part of an art teacher. Her blonde hair is gathered on top of her head, held together with a couple of paint brushes. She has on a pair of black square-rimmed glasses. This is the first time I've ever seen her wear glasses. Her apron and skinny jeans are covered in smudges of paint and clay. Lucky scans the class as she explains what techniques she'll be teaching us, her eyes narrow when her gaze lands on us.

"Hi, Lucky," Lucy and I call out in unison while waving.

She mouths a "fuck me" as she drops her head, trying to refocus before telling the class to turn on their wheels and to play with the clay to gain a feel for it. Lucy and I flip the switch and the wheels spin to life. I dip my fingers into my bowl of water and carefully press them into the clay as it spins around.

Lucky slowly walks along each row, stopping to show the other students how to mold their clay into a simple bowl. It's fun to see her in her element. Sure, that night in the club she looked like she was having fun up on stage, but here she's looking relaxed and happy.

"What the hell are you two doing here?" Lucky barks, stopping right in front of us. "Brooke, I thought you were leaving for the islands with Brian today, and Lucy, aren't you supposed to be working at the shop?"

"Brian's still sleeping off his shift and my assistant manager is taking care of the shop," Lucy slurs. "We wanted to have a little fun and learn how to make some clay pots." Lucy runs her hands up along the clay. Her clay pot looking a little more phallic than pot.

"We just wanted to watch you in your real element. If you want us to leave, we will."

"No, please stay. Let me make one last round then I'll come sit with you guys." She reluctantly gives in.

A few minutes later Lucky takes a seat at the wheel next to me and starts on her own project. "Well, I see Lucy is making a giant penis. What are you making Brooke?"

"It's supposed to be a bowl. Thought I could give it to Brian to put his keys in." I press my fingers on the inside of my sad little bowl, working the clay up to form the sides.

"Speaking of Brian, how are things going between you two?"

"Things with us are so great. He makes me so damn happy." I can't hold back the huge smile that's lighting up my face.

"Oh Brooke, that's so awesome. I'm really happy for you two." Lucy smiles up from her wheel. "Okay, so now here's the real question. How happy does he make you in the sack?" Lucy asks, her voice echoing in the tiny classroom. A few of the students glance back at us. I shyly smile and try to hide my face.

"She's been drinking hasn't she? She only gets mouthy about sex when she's had a few."

"Yeah, we stopped for lunch and ordered a pitcher of margaritas, and before I noticed, she'd downed half a pitcher before our food had even arrived."

"Bailey must be with Colton's family this weekend? She only gets that sloshed when Bailey's not with her." She laughs, shaking her head. "But please answer the question, I'm rather curious, too."

I can feel my face flush and my fingers stumble along my clay bowl, warping the rim. I let out a soft sigh. "He's fucking amazing. Like mind-blowingly good. Sex with Jake was always great. He was into the whole bondage scene and that was fun and all. But God, sex with Brian is so fucking intense. I can't keep my hands or my mouth off of him." I pinch my thighs together, feeling the heat beginning to pool. Just talking about him gets me all hot and bothered. "We can't go five minutes without wanting to climb on top of each other. We went for a ride on the Ferris wheel on our first date. The damn thing got stuck, and so to kill the time while they fixed it, we fucked in our dark little pod," I admit.

"No fucking way!" Lucky's hands fumble from her shock making her clay pot rip into pieces. "You fucked on the Ferris wheel? Brooke, you're an adventurous little minx. I haven't even fucked on that yet."

"And we also did it at his precinct. I couldn't help it, he's been working the night shift and I've been so fucking horny. Not even my vibrator can get me off like Brian can."

"Damn Brooke, I'm liking you more and more." Lucky flashes me an approving sideways grin. "I've always wondered this . . . so uh, how's Brian in the penis department?"

I pull my lip between my teeth. My breathing growing deep and shallow, breasts heaving under my apron as I picture Brian's big beautiful perfect cock. "It's the most stunning, long, thick, perfect cock I've ever seen," I softly moan. My mind wandering back to this morning. Me on my knees sucking his delicious cock. I could spend every day devouring his cock. I feel myself starting to get a little too overheated and I splash a little water on my face.

"Lucky, I've seen Brian naked before and let me tell ya, Brooke is one very lucky girl," Lucy chimes in. And Lucky and I both glare over at her.

"When have you seen Brian naked?" we both ask in unison.

"It was at our high school graduation party at my house. I accidentally walked in on him while he was changing into his swimming trunks," she says matter-of-factly. "He has nothing on my Colton."

"Oh, here we go again." Lucky rolls her eyes and goes back to trying to fix her clay pot.

"My Colton was a ten-inch dream machine. The first time we had sex he had to go down on me for like an hour to get me relaxed enough to take a dick that big." Lucy looks longingly at her clay statue and I think I might need to take it away from her before she jumps on top of it and takes it for a test drive. "That's one of the things I miss about that man. I haven't found any man that can come close to Colton in that department."

Wow! This is the most Lucy has divulged about Colton since we met. All she'd told me was that he was in the Army and that he died when the bomb he was disarming went off.

Note to self—Get Lucy hammered more often.

"I miss those big browns of his. His sweet little dimples when he smiles, and the way he'd pull my hair and call me his dirty little buttercup when we fucked." She lets out a heavy sigh and starts seductively running her hands up and down her clay statue that is looking more and more like a penis. The two men sitting next to her watch in wonder and probably wish she was doing that to them. She looks over at the two men, still working her clay up and down. "So boys, how are those bowls coming along?" She winks and just then her clay statue limps over in her hands. "Well, that's disappointing," she pouts, holding the lifeless clay in her hands.

I like drunk Lucy.

* * *

I help Lucy into her bed, covering her up with a blanket as she passes out. I leave her a glass of water on the nightstand and give her a light kiss on the forehead before turning to head downstairs to make sure I packed everything Lola will need while we're gone. Lucy volunteered to watch Lola while Brian and I are at his cabin. I reach the bottom of the stairs to find Lola cornering Lucky in the living room, growling at her.

"Lola, no!" I shout. "Leave Lucky alone." I run into the kitchen and jump between Lola and Lucky.

"That damn dog is fucking crazy." Lucky gives Lola the evil eye as Lola toddles off to her bed by the fireplace.

"She's a good girl, she just has issues with people sometimes." I kneel down to Lola and give her a few rubs behind her ears. "You be a good girl, Lola. No biting poor Lucky, okay?"

"So is drunk-o finally passed out up there? I can't believe

you're leaving me here with princess drinks-a-lot and horn dog Ryder all week," Lucky groans.

"You'll be just fine, Lucky. Lucy needed to let off a little steam. You would too if you were a single working mom." I give Lola a kiss on the top of her head. I stand back up and walk over to the kitchen to finish unpacking Lola's food and bowls. "Let Lucy know I put Lola's food in the pantry, and we'll be back next Sunday night. I better go, Brian will be getting up soon."

I start to head for the door when I hear Lucky mumble something behind me. "What was that Lucky?"

"Before you go there's something I want to say to you," she says, looking down at her hands. "I'm shitty with emotions and telling people how I feel so bear with me for a sec."

Quiet, shy Lucky, this is a first.

One thing Lucky's good at is expressing herself. It's strange to see her struggling to find the right words.

"What is it Lucky?"

"That day at the lake I wanted to tell you how much you mean to me since you've come into my life. But again feelings are hard for me to convey so I kept my mouth shut. I know I bust balls, crack jokes, and tease you sometimes, but you really have become one of my best friends, and I'm so glad you and Brian have found each other. He's been lost and hurting for so long, I'm glad to finally see him happy with you."

"Wow, thanks, Lucky. That's the sweetest thing you've ever said to me." I start to tear up a little at her words. I knew under that hard exterior she has a heart of gold.

"Okay, don't start getting all mushy on me. I don't do tears either. Now suck it up and go enjoy your week of hot animal sex." She slaps me on the ass then ushers me out the door.

There's the Lucky I know and love.

CHAPTER TWENTY-THREE

Brian

"IS THIS ALL YOU ARE bringing?" I ask, taking the small black backpack from Brooke so she can lock her door. I'm used to traveling with my sister and my mom, who would bring everything in their closets for a three-day trip.

"I only packed what I really need and figure with you around, I won't be needing much clothing." She smiles at me over her shoulder. Damn right she's not going to need much clothing. If I have my way, she'll be naked all the time.

"Where's your stuff?" she asks, looking for my bag.

"I keep an extra set of clothes at the cabin just in case I ever need to get away. Well, since you packed light we can take the bike I've just finished restoring. I've been dying to take her out on the road." I slide my hand into Brooke's and we walk down the hallway to elevator.

"Wait you have more than one?"

"I have three in storage here in the building. I've been restoring vintage bikes since I was fifteen. My uncle took me to the salvage yard on my birthday and he bought me an empty shell of a classic nineteen sixty-eight Triumph T120. We spent all summer bringing her back to life. I drove that bike for three years then it got stolen during my freshman year at UW. But the passion to restore old bikes has stuck with me."

As soon as we reach the far corner of the garage where I store my bikes Brooke's hand slips from mine. She stares intensely at the black and red motorcycle, running her fingers along the leather seat and up along the eyebrow tank.

"Is this a 1969 Triumph Bonneville?" The moment the words slip from her lips, I feel myself getting a little hard. Not only is she smart, beautiful, and great in the sack, she also knows about classic motorcycles. I think I've died and gone to heaven.

"It is. It took me three years and a lot of late nights to bring this old girl back to life," I say with a prideful smile. "How do you know about vintage bikes?"

"My brother's best friend in college collected vintage bikes, and he used to take me for rides when they'd come home for the summer."

"I bet he gave you quite the ride," I reply, feeling a pang of jealousy. I slide Brooke's backpack on and climb onto the leather seat.

"Hey, it was nothing like that. He was twenty-one and I was sixteen. He was just being nice to me. Besides, even if I was old enough, he still wasn't my type."

"Oh yeah, and what is your type?"

"Hot police officers named Brian Gamble." She winks and climbs on behind me, wrapping her arms around my waist. I smile to myself at her response.

The roar of the engine echoes through the quiet garage. Brooke's arms squeeze me tighter as we pull out into traffic.

An hour and a half later we pull onto the ferry were we park and get off the bike. . I follow Brooke up the stairs to the main deck. My eyes locked on the plump curve of her ass the whole way up. Before Brooke I was a full on tit man, but she has an ass that could bring a man to his knees.

The boat's pretty packed with tourists and weekenders

heading to the islands. We find a quiet spot by the railing with a perfect view of the sun setting in the distance. This is the first time I've brought anyone to my place on Orcas Island. It is my sanctuary, my place to escape the world, and where I can be alone. It's the first time in years, I don't want to be alone. I want to share this place with someone. I want to share it with Brooke.

Brooke's quickly becoming a first in a lot of things for me lately. The first woman to call me out on all my shit, the first to sleep in my bed, and the first I've said, 'I love you' to and really meant it. I'm looking forward to seeing what other firsts are in store for us.

"It's so bonkers beautiful out here." Brooke finally breaks the silence.

"Not as beautiful as you." I slide my hands around her waist and softly kiss her cheek.

"When did you become so sweet?" she asks, reaching her hand back and running her fingers through my hair.

"You must bring it out in me." I dip my head down, lips ghosting over her neck and I whisper, "I can't wait to get you to my cabin and into my bed. I've been aching to be inside you all fucking week." A satisfied grin pulls at my lips when I hear her take a deep breath. The little hairs on the back of her neck standing on end with anticipation. I love the effect I have on her, barely even touching her, and her body's already springing to life.

The ferry pulls up to the dock at Orcas Island. We climb back on my bike and drive along the hilly road that leads up to my cabin. The headlight illuminates the tiny red barn style cabin as we roll up. The cabin is nestled among tall evergreen trees, and my nearest neighbor is two miles away. It's quiet and peaceful and the perfect getaway when I need to clear my head.

Climbing off my bike, I grab Brooke's hand and lead us up

the stairs to the front door. I open the door, letting Brooke step inside first. Flipping on the kitchen light, I watch as Brooke gets the lay of the land. In the back, there's just the bedroom and bathroom, then a small living room that opens to the kitchen. It's small, but it suits me just fine.

"I know it's a little small."

"It's perfect, Brian." She turns to face me, giving me her sweet smile.

"You really like it?" I set her bag on the couch and step closer to her, sliding my arms around her.

"I love it. It could be an old rundown shack and I'd still love it because you're here." She grins, wrapping her arms around my neck she gently kisses me. I lift her up in my arms and carry her into the bedroom and set her down on her feet. I've been waiting all week to get her all to myself, and I can't wait a minute longer.

She pushes me down onto the bed then takes a few steps back, kicking off her pink Chucks, she turns her back to me, and pulls off her shirt. She looks over her shoulder, a sultry glint in her eyes as she unhooks her bra, slowly sliding the straps down and then tossing it over her shoulder—it lands over my head. I press the lace against my nose, breathing in her sweet intoxicating scent. I can feel my dick already straining against my jeans.

I hear the sound of the zipper on her pants. She teases me by slowly sliding them down, bending at the hips, giving me an excellent view of her gorgeous ass. As soon as she steps out of her jeans I grab her by the hips and pull her into my lap. "Such a fucking little tease," I growl in her ear, grinding her hips against me and letting her feel how hard she's making me. I slide a hand between her legs, gently stroking her through her already damp panties. "So fucking wet. I bet you've been thinking about my dick fucking this tight little pussy of yours all day, huh?"

A whispered, 'yes' escapes her lips, her head dropping back against my shoulder. Her hips grind harder with need, and my lap is now wet with her desire. She's so fucking ready for me, but I'm not going to give her what she wants just yet.

"Lay on the bed and take off your panties," I order.

She does as she's told and climbs onto the bed. Laying back on the blankets, she slides off her panties and tosses them at me, giving me mischievous little grin. "Such a little brat!" I pull my shirt over my head. Brooke watches me undress with dark hungry eyes as a hand finds its way to her wet little cunt and her fingers circle along her clit as I slide off my jeans. She looks so damn sexy.

"I don't remember giving you permission to touch your pussy."

"You didn't," she says giving me a cocky grin. "What are you going to do about it, Officer?" she challenges.

I walk over to my closet and pull out my spare set of handcuffs. Brooke's eyes widen as I dangle the metal cuffs over her.

"You found out my weakness," she purrs.

"Ace, do you like being tied up?"

She nods yes offering her hands up to me. She is full of surprises. I grab her left hand and lock the metal cuff around her wrist. Bringing her hand up to the bedpost, I lace the other cuff around it and then restrain her other wrist. Once she's where I want her, I climb up on the bed and kneel next to her.

Brooke twists her wrists and lets out a squeal of excitement. "Now that should hold you, naughty girl," I say grinning down at her. My hand glides down her chest, my finger flicks over her rosy pink nipple and I pinch her taut bud between my fingers.

"More," she softly demands. I'm all too happy to oblige, tweaking her other nipple, then back to the first one, repeating this until they are bright red and she's bowing off the bed. I lean over her and place a gentle kiss on each of her nipples before continuing down her body until I'm nestled between her legs.

Oh, how I've missed her body. Drifting past where she wants my mouth the most, I grab her left ankle and bring her leg up while placing feather light kisses along her calf.

Brooke's moans turning to giggles when I gently stroke the underside of her knee. Someone's ticklish—I will have to remember that for later. Moving down her inner thigh, Brooke's greedy hips arch up begging for my mouth to be on her juicy wet cunt. Instead, I pin her legs and run my middle finger down along her dripping wet slit, circling her swollen bud.

Brooke's hands strain against the cuffs. Her chest heaves in rhythm with her deep haggard breaths. She looks so fucking sexy cuffed to my bed, spread open, dripping wet and begging for me. Circling her opening with the pad of my finger, her hips buck against my hand.

"Brian, please I need you," she pleads.

"Tell me what you want, Ace." I swirl the tip of my finger inside her.

"I want your cock. Please Brian, I fucking need it."

"Since you asked so nicely," I growl. Pushing her legs wide with my knees, I grip the base of my cock and push just the tip inside her. Her greedy cunt squeezing around me. I pull out and tease her opening before pushing inside her again, just giving her an inch more.

Brooke is writhing and begging, her hips rolling and desperate for more as her hands pull even harder at the cuffs. With her body desperate for release, I continue my sweet torture, inching inside her then pulling out until she's screaming for me to make her fucking come.

"I fucking love when you beg." I grip her hips and thrust deep inside her, finally giving her what she wants . . . what she needs. She's so tight and wet, I could almost come just from her pussy throbbing around me. I begin to work myself in and out of her, watching as my cock comes out covered in her sweet juices then disappearing back inside her.

Enveloping her body with mine, our fingers lacing, I press my forehead to hers, and hold her in my gaze while I draw out every thrust wanting this moment to last forever.

Brooke's eyes flutter closed. "Open your eyes, Brooke. I want to see you come. You look so beautiful when you come."

With each deep thrust, the fire begins to build deep inside me. And I can feel Brooke pulsating all around me, moaning and chanting my name like a prayer, and it's the most beautiful thing I've ever seen.

"So damn beautiful." Sliding my arms under her, I hold her tight against me. I can feel the emptiness I'd been feeling all week fade away as we make love, reclaiming each other. Brooke's head rolls back as she finally let's go, each pulse and squeeze of her pussy pulling me right along with her. Making me come hard.

I lay on top of her, still holding her in my arms, not wanting to let her go but I know she's ready to get out of those cuffs. I reluctantly pull out of her and climb out of bed to grab the key to the handcuffs. After releasing her wrists, I kiss and rub each one then pull her into my arms. It feels so fucking good to have her back in my arms where she belongs. It makes me feel whole again.

CHAPTER TWENTY-FOUR

Brooke

THE MORNING SUN BEGINS CREEPING in through the windows filling Brian's bedroom with a soft glow that stirs me awake. I find Brian's head nestled on my right breast and his hand firmly planted on my left breast. I can listen to his deep breaths as he sleeps peacefully snaked around me. He's so damn cute. My sexy alpha cop reduced to mush by my amazing rack. I giggle to myself and give him a gentle kiss on the top of his head.

Running my fingers through his hair while my mind wanders back to last night I feel a slight ache in my wrists. I notice a faint red line circling the skin of my left hand and a familiar ache builds between my legs as I remember being cuffed to the bed and Brian torturing me in the most delicious way possible.

I use to love when Jake would tie me up during sex. He opened me up to a whole new sexual world, but that was always my favorite. I use to be a major control freak, being able to let someone else take away the control was freeing. I never thought I would ever feel that kind of safety again, but when I saw Brian bring out those cuffs, I knew I could trust him. He can cuff me to the bed anytime.

Brian rubs his face along my breast before looking up at me

with those gorgeous sparkling brown eyes. "Good morning, Ace." He grins, placing a kiss on my each of my nipples.

"Good morning, baby. Did you sleep well?" I ask with a sigh as he flicks his tongue across my nipple.

"I slept amazing, but I always do when you're in my bed." Brian shifts his weight over me, nestles between my legs, and rubs his hard length along my growing wet slit.

"What's on the agenda for today?" I softly moan.

"After I make love to my girl . . ." He aligns himself at my entrance then slowly pushes inside me. "I thought we could go into town and have breakfast." He accentuates every word with a slow deep thrust. "Maybe go for a hike." Dips his tongue between my breasts. "Or we could just stay in bed all day." He runs his tongue up along my neck.

"Mmm, I choose bed."

⋆ ⋆ ⋆

Brian and I walk down the crowded streets after reluctantly coming out of our happy little bubble when our hunger for food overtook our hunger for each other. We walk along the rows of little boutiques and quaint restaurants hand in hand. I'm feeling so at peace. After saying a final goodbye to Jake, it felt like a giant weight had been lifted off my shoulders. Jake would always be a special and big part of my life, but now I felt like it was finally okay to move forward with my life, and I hope it will always include Brian.

We find a quiet corner booth in a small cafe right on the water. The sun's sparkling off the clear blue water, and we can see people out in their boats enjoying the first sunny spring day. After the waitress takes our order, Brian and I settle back in the booth snuggled up close to each other and steal kisses when no one's looking.

"It's so beautiful. How long have you been coming here?" I ask.

"Since I was a kid. Started with my dad bringing us here every summer, then after he passed away, my mom kept the tradition alive."

"It's nice that your mom continued to do that."

"She tried to keep his memory alive in any way she could. Whenever we were here, it felt like he was here with us."

Brian looks out at the water, becoming a little quiet with talk of his dad. I can tell talking about his dad is hard for him. I was the same way when it came to talking about my mom. It's tough losing a parent at such a young age.

"How long have you had a place here?" I ask changing the subject.

"I bought the land about four years ago and finished building the cabin last year." He turns his attention back to me, the somber look in his eyes fading away.

"Did you do all the work yourself?"

"I did. I spent every weekend here working on it. It was very therapeutic for me actually." That's when I realize he must have bought the property after his break up with Jillian. "You're actually the first person I've brought here," he admits.

"Are you serious? You haven't even brought Ryder here?" I ask trying to hide my surprise.

"Not even Ryder has been here. For the longest time, I've wanted to keep this my private sanctuary. My escape. You're the first person I've wanted to share this with." He hides his shy smile behind his coffee.

"Brian, I don't know what to say." My face lights up almost brighter than the sun. I can't believe he chose me to share this with. I feel so honored. "Thank you, it means a lot to me that you'd share this special place with me." I grab his coffee mug from his hand and cup his face in my hands and softly kiss him.

"It feels good to have you here with me and last night was incredible." He brings my hand up to his mouth and places a soft kiss on the back of my hand. "Have you always liked being tied up?"

"I didn't know I liked it until I met Jake. He kind of showed me a lot of things I didn't know I would like." I can see Brian getting a little uncomfortable at the mention of Jake, "I'm sorry if talking about Jake is making you uncomfortable."

"No it's fine, I want to know everything about you and that includes your life with Jake. Please continue," he urges.

"When I met Jake I was in a really bad place, I had just dropped out of medical school and ran away to New York to be closer to my brother, Hunter. I was floundering until Jake stepped in and helped me put my life back together. He encouraged me to start writing again, and he helped me find myself. He opened me up to love. I think, in a way, he was preparing me to meet you. Had we met any earlier I wouldn't have been open to us. If that makes sense." I feel like I'm just rambling.

"No, I completely understand. After Jillian, I was a complete mess. I would have used you and threw you out like all the other women that came before you. A woman as wonderful as you deserves better than that. I needed to get her out of my system before I could even imagine being worthy of someone like you."

"You are more than worthy of my heart, Brian Gamble."

* * *

After breakfast, Brian and I picked up a few groceries from the farmer's market then walked along the East Sound back to his cabin. Brian filled me in on all the activities we could do around the island, but I would be happy if we just stayed locked away in his cabin.

I've just finished putting away the food we purchased when Brian comes out from his bedroom carrying a small black gun case and a box of ammo.

"What are you doing with that?" I ask curiously.

"I thought it might be fun to teach my girl how to shoot."

He looks so cute and excited by the idea, I don't have the heart to tell him I already know how to shoot. Being the only daughter of a cop, he made sure I knew how to protect myself.

"That sounds like fun."

I follow Brian outside behind the cabin. He nails up a silhouette target on one of the trees that's about a hundred yards from the house. He opens the gun case, revealing two 9mm Glock's and two full clips. I'm very familiar with this caliber of gun, it being the first gun my dad taught me how to use when I was sixteen.

Brian loads one of the clips into the gun then walks around behind me. He hands me the weapon with the safety still on, then grips my hips, and tells me to widen my stance a bit. He presses up nice and tight against my back and slides his hands down along my arms. I can see he really wants to teach me how to fire a gun. He helps me steady my aim as I bring the gun up level with the target. He takes off the safety and warns me about the kickback. "Now just gently squeeze the trigger," he says, his breath hot against my neck.

I squeeze the trigger firing off a shot square in the chest of the target. Brian takes a step back and stares wide-eyed at the target. "Wow! Now that was an impressive shot for a newbie."

"Well, I do have a confession to make." I bring the gun down to my side and turn to him. "I already know how to fire a gun."

"What? Why didn't you say so?" I can hear the disappointment in his voice.

"You looked so excited about teaching me, I didn't have the

heart to tell you I already know how to shoot," I say with a sheepish grin.

"Well then, show me what you got, Ace." He steps back behind me, watching as I bring the gun back up. Lining up my shot, I squeeze the trigger, firing the full clip into the target in quick succession. Once the clip is empty, I bring the gun down and admire my handy work. Five perfect shots into the heart.

Brian stands silently staring at the target. I'm wondering what's going through his mind right now.

"Normally I'd be slightly intimidated by how good a shot you are, but I'm actually rather turned on right now."

I giggle to myself when I see the growing bulge in his jeans. I set the gun back into the case then walk back over to Brian. I slide my hand down the front of his jeans. He's so fucking hard. "We shouldn't let this go to waste," I murmur, feeling the adrenaline coursing through my body.

He grabs me roughly by the arms and swings me around, pressing me up against the wall of the cabin. We both make quick work of unbuttoning each other's pants. His lips capture mine in a deep rough kiss, his greedy tongue devouring my mouth while his hands yank my pants down off my hips. He whips out his hard length, giving it a few tugs before thrusting hard into me. My cries of pleasure echo through the forest air as he pounds relentlessly into my slick cunt.

He nuzzles his face in the crook of my neck, sucking and biting my tender flesh, marking me like I'm his fucking territory. And I am. I'm all his to use in any way he sees fit. This man owns me, mind, body, and soul.

His thrusts become wild and erratic as he takes me harder and faster, hitting me with both pleasure and pain. With one final hard snap of his hips, my body shudders as we both come. Pleasure ripping through us both. He slows his pace filling me with every last drop of him and it's sweet and hot.

His body finally stills, his ragged breath calming as he tenderly kisses the red marks that he's left in his wild wake on my neck. His hands slide down along my thighs lifting me up, keeping himself firmly seated inside me as he carries me back inside for round two.

CHAPTER TWENTY-FIVE

Brian

"ACE, TIME TO WAKE UP." I sweep the hair from Brooke's face and gently kiss her cheek and rub her back. She cracks an eye open and pouts when she sees that I'm already up and fully dressed.

"Why are you dressed, and what time is it?" she sleepily groans.

"It's seven, and we have a party to get to."

"Seven in the morning? Who throws a party at seven in the morning?"

"It's my mom's birthday, and we have a very long ferry ride to her house." I've wanted to introduce Brooke to my mom and my sister for a while now and when I got the invitation to her birthday party, I figured it would be the perfect time for Brooke to meet them.

Brooke's eyes spring open and she jumps up in bed. "Your mom's birthday? You want me to meet your mom? Your mom! Brian, I didn't pack anything to meet a mom in. I didn't even pack my makeup or my curling iron. Your mom!" she shouts.

Brooke's eyes are burning with panic and she's mumbling incoherently to herself. I quickly realize I should have brought meeting my mom up a little earlier, but I didn't want to send her screaming for the door. I rest my hands on her shoulders trying to calm her nerves.

"Brooke it doesn't matter what you wear. My mom is going to love you." I try to reassure her, but it's not going over very well.

Her eyes narrow, staring me down like daggers. I can almost see the smoke coming out of her ears. Okay, maybe I should just keep my mouth shut.

"Are you insane? Everything I brought is either lingerie or screams *I'm only wearing this so your son will fuck me later.*" Her breathing is deep and angry, and I'm slightly afraid she going to lunge at me and strangle me to death. But I'm a highly trained cop and I've dealt with crazier.

"I'm sorry, Ace. I should've told you sooner that I wanted you to meet my mom. How about this, we head into town, grab some breakfast, then we can go shopping so you can pick out something you can wear to my mom's. And I'll pay," I suggest, trying to put out the fire.

The insane panic begins to fade from Brooke's eyes as she contemplates my suggestions. "Okay. But next time you pull a stunt like this, I will rip your balls off."

"Believe me, I won't do this again." I raise my hands up in surrender. "Oh, and by the way, you could wear a paper bag, and I'd still want to rip you out of it and fuck you."

Brooke tries to stifle a laugh. Her lips form a thin line hiding her smile. "Don't try and make me laugh, you're still in the dog house."

"Oh, come on Ace, let me make it up to you?" I lean in ready to win her over with a kiss that will make her forget all about my stupidity, but I'm met with the palm of her hand in my face pushing me away.

"Down boy," she scolds, climbing out of bed and out of my reach. She struts naked into the bathroom slamming the door behind her, leaving me and my erection to fend for ourselves.

Yep, I'm officially an ass.

★ ★ ★

Sitting in the chair of shame outside the dressing rooms, I flip through my phone checking for the score of last night's Mariners game, while Brooke tries on every dress the store fucking has. She's definitely laying on the torture nice and thick, first not letting me kiss her, then not letting me hold her hand during our walk from the cabin to the restaurant. She knows my weaknesses and she's using every last one to prove her point. And it's fucking working. I'm dying inside, my hands are aching to touch her, lips desperate for a taste of her beautiful full lips. I'm like an addict in desperate need of a fix.

"I think I've found the perfect one," she calls out from behind the curtain.

"Thank God," I whisper under my breath, relieved that this round of torture is finally over.

Brooke draws back the curtain and takes my breath away when I see her dressed in a white, short, strapless dress embellished with little birds and a whisper of pink lace and tulle running around the hem. Her shoulders are covered in a light pink cardigan with tiny crystals along the collar. She looks like an angel.

"Brooke, you look beautiful." I drink in every inch of her as she does a little turn to show me the full look of the dress.

"Do you think so?" she asks, smoothing her hands down the skirt and looking over at me with nervous eyes.

"You're taking my breath away, Ace."

She smiles, then motions for me to come closer. Grabbing my hands, she wraps my arms around her waist. "You're out of the dog house now," she says, freeing me from my punishment. Standing up on her tiptoes, she snakes her arms around my neck and softly kisses me. Finally giving me what I've been craving all damn morning. I deepen our kiss, pushing my tongue into her mouth.

The sales girl ruins our moment when she comes back to check on Brooke. She gives us a knowing glare before asking Brooke how the dresses are working for her. Brooke hands the sales girl the tags from her dress so I can pay while she gives herself one last once over before we leave for the ferry.

On the way to the dock, Brooke picks out a fresh bouquet of white and pink peonies for my mom. I can tell she's still nervous about meeting Mom, but she has nothing to worry about, my mom is going to love her . . . purely because I love her.

CHAPTER TWENTY-SIX

Brooke

THE WHOLE FERRY RIDE TO Bainbridge Island the nervous butterflies flutter around in my stomach. I can't believe Brian just sprung meeting his mom on me like that. Not giving me any time to mentally prepare myself. I'm usually okay with meeting parents, but for some reason meeting Brian's mom has me in such a state I almost want to throw up over the side of the boat. Brian's the only son in his family, and after dealing with Jake's overly possessive mother, I'm a little wary of going through the same thing with Brian's mom.

As we walked up the path to the house, the butterflies turn to knots, but as soon as Brian's mom meets us at the front door my nerves begin to settle, much in the same way as being around Brian has done for me.

She's dressed conservatively in a pair of blue slacks with a blue floral blouse and a white cardigan. Her chestnut brown hair is perfectly pulled back into a low ponytail. Her brown eyes sparkle with joy when she sees the both of us.

"Oh, my sweet boy, it's so good to see you." She pulls Brian in for a quick hug before turning her attention to me. "This must be the beautiful Brooke I've heard so much about." I'm taken aback when she wraps her arms around me, giving me a warm, welcoming hug.

"It's so nice to meet you, Mrs. Gamble," I say, returning her hug.

"Oh sweetheart, please call me Eliana." She hugs me tighter and I already love her. "Mrs. Gamble is my mother-in-law."

"How is Grandma by the way?" Brian asks as Eliana leads us up the walk way to her home.

"Still alive and kicking. That old bat is going to outlive us all." She grins back at us. "I've got to go check on Uncle Charlie and make sure he's not burning the ribs. You two make yourselves comfortable, and Brooke, I look forward to chatting with you later."

The brown-shingled two-story house is set up on a hill flanked by tall evergreen trees with windows that overlook the well-manicured property. The flowerbeds are bursting with blooms in every color in of the rainbow. I can't believe this is where Brian grew up.

Steeping inside the house, my senses are overtaken by the smells of baking cookies, and the barbecue that's being cooked on the large grill out on the back deck. The interior is beautifully decorated in warm brown and cream colors, with splashes of rich burgundy in the form of oriental rugs and throw pillows. There is a fire roaring in the river rock fireplace and the walls are covered in family photographs.

Brian ushers me through the house to the big open kitchen, and the nervous butterflies come back when we walk out onto the back deck, and see the backyard is filled with Brian's aunts, uncles, and his little cousins playing on the jungle gym and in the sandbox. It's one thing to meet his mom, but now it looks like I'm meeting his entire family.

I think I'm going to throw up.

I squeeze Brian's hand tighter as I look across the sea of new faces. Just then I hear little voices shout out for Brian. I turn to see two bright-eyed, blonde little girls come bounding up the stairs onto the deck and running straight for him. Brian kneels down opening his arms for them and they practically knock him over, jumping into his arms. They can't be older than seven. They're dressed in matching pink and purple princess dresses, with tiaras resting on top of their curly hair.

"Hey girls, try not to break your Uncle Brian," a voice calls out from behind me. I turn and spot who I can only assume is Brian's sister, Natalie. She pretty much looks like a female version of Brian except she has long blonde hair.

"You must be the famous Brooke we've heard so much about." She smiles, walking over to us. "Wow big brother, bold move bringing her here to meet our big crazy family. I hope she doesn't run off screaming by the end of the night," she teases.

Brian stands up and gives his sister a side hug. Both his little nieces still cling to his legs. "If she can survive one night with our family then she can survive anything."

"It's so nice to meet you, Brooke." She extends her hand, and I shake it gently. "And these two little princesses are Sophia and Chloe. Girls, this is Brooke, Uncle Brian's girlfriend."

"Hi Brooke, I'm Princess Sophie." The green-eyed little girl smiles up at me and holds her hand out for me to shake.

I kneel down and shake Sophie's hand. "It's nice to meet you, Princess Sophie." I look over at Chloe, who's hiding behind Brian's legs. The shy one I'm guessing. I give Chloe a small wave when she peaks her head out, and she returns my wave with a timid smile. They are both absolutely adorable.

"Brooke, do you like tea parties?" Sophie asks.

"It just so happens I love tea parties."

"Do you want to come join us for one right now? Daddy bought us a new tea set with Anna and Elsa from Frozen, and Mommy got us Frozen cupcakes to have with our tea." She grins excitedly.

"Sophie, why don't you take Uncle Brian to your tea party for now? Mommy wants to get to know Brooke for a bit, then we'll come join you later."

"Okay, Mommy. Come on, Uncle Brian." Sophie grabs Brian's hand and starts to pull him toward the stairs.

"Will you be okay?" he turns and asks.

"She'll be just fine." Natalie pushes Brian out of the way, and I see Brian mouth, "Be nice" before disappearing down the stairs.

Natalie turns to me, loops her arm through mine, and leads me over to the bar. "You look like you could use a drink. How about a glass of wine?"

"That would be great, thank you."

Natalie reaches behind the bar, grabbing a bottle of red wine and two wine glasses. I follow her over to an empty table by the railing at the edge of the deck where we can see everyone below us talking and laughing. She pours us both a hardy glass of wine, then takes a seat across from me.

I grab my glass and take a long slow sip. I down almost half the wine in one go, hoping the wine will help calm my nerves a bit. "That's much better, thank you. Brian kind of sprung this on me this morning, so I haven't really had much time to prepare for meeting his entire family."

Natalie rolls her eyes, letting out a disapproving sigh. "My idiot brother hasn't been in a relationship for so long, he's forgotten you have to give a girl at least a week to prepare themselves for meeting the family. Especially ours. We can be a bit intense." She takes a sip of her wine then relaxes back in her chair. "I will warn you, you are the first girl Brian has brought home to meet us since his girlfriend in high school. So you'll be inundated by our aunts asking you a million questions and probably hugging you to death."

"Brian never brought Jillian here to meet all of you?" That

seems surprising to me considering Lucy told me Brian was ready to propose to Jillian before he caught her cheating.

"I had the misfortune of meeting her right after they started dating. She put on a good front of being a nice person, but I could see right through her. I tried to warn Brian about her, but Brian, of course, didn't listen, and well, you know how that ended." She pauses taking another sip of her wine like she needed to clean Jillian's name from her tongue. "I think in some ways he subconsciously knew things weren't going to work out between them, so he didn't want to introduce her to our mom, which makes me believe he sees a future with you." She winks at me over the rim of her wine glass.

I hope she's right. The past few days at Brian's cabin have made me fall even harder for him. I'm starting to see a future with him, too. My anger about Brian surprising me with meeting his family fades away and is replaced with joy that he brought me here and not Jillian.

Natalie and I proceed to polish off our bottle of wine. Natalie filling me in on all the embarrassing stories of Brian as a kid. I especially enjoyed the story of Brian and Ryder getting busted for streaking at the homecoming game when they were in high school. Double trouble for sure.

Natalie works from home as a graphic designer so she can be home with Sophie and Chloe. She's also the first to break the family cop mold and married a firefighter.

Natalie's husband, Kyle, calls her away for a minute to help set up the kids pool. I pan the backyard for Brian and his nieces, spotting them over by the castle playhouse sitting at the little table. I get up and walk over to join them. As I get closer, I can see that the girls have managed to get Brian to put on a sparkly tiara and a bright pink feathered boa. They have him completely wrapped around their little fingers, and it's cute as hell. He sits there sipping tea and munching on a cupcake, being the good sweet uncle.

Seeing this, I start thinking about how good of a father he will be, so loving and protective. I've never really thought about having kids before. Jake and I were so focused on our careers; the thought of kids never entered our minds. But now, seeing Brian with his nieces, I have this overwhelming urge to scream out, *Put your baby in me!*

Brian catches me watching them, and his face turns a bright shade of red. He pulls off his tiara and boa and starts to get up from the table. "Excuse me ladies, but I need to go spend some time with Princess Brooke." Brian saunters over to me, eyeing me up and down. I love the way he looks at me, like I'm the only woman in the world. It makes me feel so beautiful and wanted. He slides his hands around my waist, stealing a kiss. I hear the girls giggling.

"Come on, I want to show you something."

Brian takes my hand and leads me into the house and upstairs to one of the bedrooms. He opens the door and ushers me inside, and it feels like we just stepped back in time. It's Brian's childhood bedroom. The walls are covered in old band posters, his twin bed sits against the back wall flanked by two windows that overlook the backyard. There are bookshelves lined with trophies and a few old books. I glance over at his dresser and see a group of framed pictures sitting on top. I walk across the room to get a better look.

Hanging above the dresser on the wall is a shadow box with a picture of who I'm assuming is Brian's dad, Matthew. He is the spitting image of his dad. Also in the box is his silver police officer's badge along with his Sergeant chevrons, his Lieutenant's bars, and his Medal of Honor. I glance down at the framed photos and one in particular catches my attention. Lifting up the wooden frame, I see it's a picture of Brian in high school, I'm guessing, wearing a baseball uniform.

"Brian, did you use to play baseball?" I ask.

Brian comes up behind me, glancing down at the picture in my hand.

"I played all through high school, and I played for the University of Washington until I blew out my rotator cuff."

I look at the Brian in the picture. He has that same sweet crooked smile painted across his face. His floppy brown hair is concealed under his baseball cap. "Brian you were so cute," I gush running my fingers over his picture.

"Really? I thought I looked gangly and nerdy."

"If we had gone to the same school, I would've had a major crush on you." I give him a playful little grin over my shoulder.

"Had a tenth-grade version of you told that kid in the picture she liked him, he would've died." He sweeps my hair to the side and starts kissing a trail of kisses down along my neck. "You know we're all alone up here." He snakes an arm around my waist pulling me tight against his hard muscular chest. My ass is brushing up against the growing bulge hidden under his jeans. "And you look so damn good in this dress."

"Brian, we're in your mother's house. What if someone comes looking for us?" I suck in a deep breath when his fingers make contact with my inner thigh.

"Brooke, we've fucked in a Ferris wheel, my precinct, and countless times outside of my cabin, and this is where you draw the line?" he says huskily. "No one is going to come up here, they're all too busy getting drunk."

"But Brian . . ."

His teasing fingers against my panties cloud my mind. His other hand moves from my waist up to my neck. His fingers wrap around my throat, gently squeezing. "But nothing. You denied me what is mine all morning. Do you know the pain you put me through by not letting me touch you? I've been aching for you all fucking day, and you're not going to keep me from having you." He squeezes my neck a little tighter and my body ignites into an intense fire.

God, I love it when he goes all alpha on me.

"Now be a good girl and take off those fucking panties and ride my fucking face until I'm drowning in you. I want to get drunk off of you before I fuck you."

He releases me then walks over to his bed and lays down on his back. I swallow hard as I set the picture back down on his dresser. I slip off my shoes then my sweater. Reaching up under my dress, I slide off my panties and walk over to the bed. I'm embarrassingly wet. He's not the only one who was aching this morning, it killed me not to feel his hands, his tongue, his body on every inch of me. But he deserved it after springing meeting his mom on me the way he did.

I straddle his face aligning myself over his full lips. Brian looks up at me with dark impatient eyes, grabs my hips, and slams me down onto his dangerously long tongue. I have to bite my lips to fight back the scream of pleasure as he pushes his tongue deep into my wet pussy. It's warm and velvety inside me. He grabs two handfuls of my ass, working me faster and harder against his mouth, devouring every inch of my pussy, and driving my body wild. I love this man's tongue. He can do things with just his tongue that can put most dicks to shame.

He's relentless, eating me out like I'm his last fucking meal. His skillful tongue working me to the brink. I brace my hands on the headboard, fighting back my moans. His scruffy beard scratches my tender flesh, his nose bumps against my swollen clit. My head is spinning, hips writhing, I'm so fucking close.

"Fuck Brian, I'm coming," I cry out as my orgasm rips through me. Brian keeps his steady, relentless pace, licking and sucking until I'm coming over and over, begging him to stop, but he doesn't until I'm a limp, exhausted mess, and he's drunk every last drop of me.

Once he's done, he grabs my hips and flips me on my back on the bed. In my daze I don't hear Brian unzip his pants. The next thing I know, Brian is thrusting his hard length deep inside my wet channel. His hand roughly pulls down the top of my dress, exposing my bare breasts. His rough hands grope and massage my tits as he pounds into me. Still sensitive from my previous orgasms, I can feel the fire building again. Brian flings my legs over his shoulders, pinning them to my chest, forcing his dick deeper inside me.

Brian lets out a primal roar as he comes. His pulsing cock sends me flying over the edge. He collapses on the bed next to me, pulling my limp body to his chest, enveloping me in his arms.

"You know, you are the first girl that's been up here," he says breaking the silence.

"Not even your high school girlfriend?"

"Nope, you are the first," he confesses.

"Natalie told me I'm the first girl you've brought home since high school."

"You are the only one worthy of meeting my family."

I smile from ear to ear at his statement. "I'm sorry for freaking out about meeting your mom and your family."

"I'm the one who is sorry for dropping this on you. I could have handled it better. I love you so much and I knew they would love you just as much as I do. I promise I will warn you next time," he says and rubs my back.

"Just a little heads up would be appreciated. But if it's going to end with awesome sex then you can surprise me anytime. You and your tongue will be the death of me." I giggle.

"Death by multiple orgasms. Best way to go in my opinion," he teases. "We better get back out there."

"I'm gonna need a minute more to collect myself. At least until the feeling comes back in my legs."

CHAPTER TWENTY-SEVEN

Brian

THE PARTY'S BEGINNING TO SETTLE down, everyone's sitting by the fire pit roasting marshmallows and sharing war stories. Brooke is sitting by my sister with Chloe and Sophie nestled right up next to her. My family's loving Brooke just as I knew they would. She's a great girl, what's not to love.

After our fun in my bedroom, we made the rounds introducing Brooke to all my aunts and uncles and my millions of cousins. She handled it all like a champ. My family can be a little intense, but Brooke turned on her charm and won everyone over like she had with me. She especially won over my nieces, showing them how to do tricks on the trampoline and drinking gallons of tea at their tea party.

"Well, there you are," I hear my mom as she comes up from behind me on the deck.

"Yeah, just needed a quiet moment. Happy Birthday by the way."

"Thank you." She joins me by the railing and follows my gaze down to Brooke. "Brooke's a very lovely girl, sweetheart. You really picked a winner with her."

"Do you really like her?" I ask, knowing my mom will be straight up with me.

"Anyone who can make you this happy is a winner in my book." She gives me a reassuring smile.

"I'm really falling hard for her, Mom. When I'm with her, I'm the happiest I've ever been, and when I'm away from her it's—"

"It's like a piece of you is missing?" she fills in the rest of my sentence.

"Yes, that. How do you know?" I ask.

"That's how I felt about your father. When we first met, we were so drawn to each other that we couldn't stand to be away from each other for very long."

"That's how I feel about Brooke. She completes me but . . ." I drop my head, hearing the familiar nagging voice in my head telling me I'm not good enough for Brooke.

"What's on your mind son?" she asks.

"It's just sometimes I don't feel like I deserve her. She's beautiful and caring and smart as hell, and I know one day she's going to realize she deserves someone better than me."

My mom slides one hand along my back and tilts my face up with the other. "You can just stop with that rubbish talk right now." She gives me a stern look. "You sound just like your father did when we first started dating. He'd go on and on about how he didn't deserve me either. It took a couple of good hits to the head of reality before he finally caught on that he was worthy."

"Really? I can't imagine Dad doubting himself on anything."

"By the time you and your sister came along he'd gotten his shit together. It took getting him away from Grandma Gamble for a couple years to have it stick. God bless that old battle-axe for trying to raise him to be a strong man, but she didn't always do it in the best of ways. He was a mess when I met him. Kind of like you are now. It took a lot of love and support on both our sides."

It's surprising to hear that my father went through the same doubts and struggles I'm going through. When I was a kid, he was always the confident cop that didn't take shit from anyone. He saw what he wanted and went after it, so to hear that he had flaws and doubts makes me feel a little better.

"Look, Brian, with every good man there's a wonderful strong woman walking side by side with them, supporting and loving him, and you have that with Brooke. She looks at you like I used to look at your father. That girl is head over heels for you. Don't let your head get in the way. You deserve to be happy with the woman you love, don't ever forget that." She leans in and gives me a kiss on the forehead. "Now get your ass down there and be with your girl."

She turns and walks down the steps to join the rest of the party. I know she's right. Brooke makes me the happiest I've ever been. She's my world and I do deserve all the love that she has to offer.

I look down at Brooke, she's smiling and laughing at something one of my uncles has said. The light from the fire dances off her beautiful face. I once heard that when you meet your soulmate they will shine brighter than anyone. I used to think that was a load of shit. That was, until I met Brooke. She's the most beautiful woman I've ever seen and, to me, she shines brighter than the sun. And I love this woman more than anything in this world. I know now without a doubt, I'm going to marry this girl.

CHAPTER TWENTY-EIGHT

Brooke

IT'S OUR LAST NIGHT AT Brian's cabin. The last night before we'll have to leave our little bubble and go back to reality. This trip has been so relaxing and amazing, I don't want it to end. I don't want to have to share my man with the rest of the world again. We spent the week exploring the island and exploring each other. I feel even more connected with Brian. He's consuming every part of me, etching himself into my soul. For the first time in two years, I finally see a future. A future with Brian. It feels so good.

After my initial panic about meeting Brian's family had subsided, I was kind of glad he surprised me with it. It kept me from stressing out and it didn't give me the opportunity to try and talk him out of taking me. Meeting Brian's Mom and family had gone off better than I could have ever hoped. His family was warm and welcoming, and Brian's Mom is such a sweetheart, I wanted to make her my mom. We'd gotten along so well, we made plans to get together for lunch the next time she came into the city. It was just a perfect day.

As I'm finishing drying the last of the dinner dishes, I hear music coming from the living room. It's one of my favorite songs 'Tennessee Whiskey' by Chris Stapleton. I shut the cabinet door, and I feel the heat of Brian come up behind me. "Come dance with me." He grabs my hand and starts to lead me to the living room.

Spinning me around, he pulls me close to his chest. This seems very un-Brian-like, but he's been full of surprises this whole trip.

"I didn't know you liked to dance." I slip my arm around his neck and lay my head against his chest as we start to sway to the music.

"I don't, but it seems like since you've come into my life you've changed my outlook on everything." He rests his head on mine. He's warm and comforting. I hear his heart beating in a calming rhythm as he takes in a deep breath. "Brooke, this past week with you has been so wonderful."

"I've loved this time with you so much, Brian. I wish it didn't have to end." I let out a sigh, wishing I could stay here and play house with Brian forever.

"Maybe it doesn't have to," he says in a hushed tone, holding me closer to him.

I lift my head up, giving him a curious look and wondering what's going on in that head of his. "What do you mean?"

"Brooke, before meeting you I was broken and drowning in darkness. I was so lost. Then you showed up at my doorstep like a bright beam of light sent to help guide me out of my personal hell." He takes in a calming breath. "You've become my best friend, my lover, and the love of my life. Every minute I'm with you I fall more and more in love with you." He looks at me with such sincerity and pure love in his eyes. Before this trip, there was a little hesitation hidden deep within his eyes, but now that's gone, replaced with confidence and love.

"When I'm not with you, it feels like a part of my soul is missing, and I never want to feel that way again. You're my world, Brooke. The love of my life and I want . . ."

My heart begins to beat rapidly in my chest. Is he about to ask what I think he's going to?

Is this all moving too fast? Do we know each other well enough? Who's to say we aren't ready for this next step. My dad married my mom within two months of meeting her. I love Brian with every ounce of my being, but am I really ready for what he's about to ask?

"I want to spend the rest of my life making you as happy as you've made me . . ." He pauses for a moment then drops to his knees. "Brooke McCoy, will you marry me?"

In that moment, all my doubts, all my hesitations fade away, and I know that I'm ready to spend the rest of my life with this man.

"Yes, Brian, I will marry you."

Brian returns to his feet and scoops me up off my mine, spinning us around the small living room. "Brooke you've made me the happiest man in the world." He sets me back down, cups my face in his strong hands, and seals our lips in a soft tender kiss.

My heart's swells with happiness and tears of joy are streaming down my face. I might have made him the happiest man alive, but he's made me the happiest woman alive. I get to marry my best friend, the love of my life and be his girl forever. There is nothing better than that.

"I don't have a ring for you yet, but as soon as we get back I'll buy you the ring of your dreams." He brings my left hand up to his mouth and kisses my ring finger.

"I don't care about the ring. I get you for the rest of my life, that's all I need. To be your wife is the greatest honor I'll ever have. I love you so much, Brian."

"I love you too, Brooke. I can't wait to make you my wife."

He lifts me off my feet again and carries me back to the bed-room, keeping his lips firmly planted on mine.

Mrs. Brian Gamble. Yeah, I like the sound of that.

CHAPTER TWENTY-NINE

Brian

"BRIAN COME ON." BROOKE PUSHES me away as I try to distract her by kissing her neck. "Your detective exam is tomorrow and you need to study."

"Brooke, we have been at this for two hours. Can't we just take a little break?" I lean back in this time, winning the battle, and trailing my lips down along her neck. I stop to suck on the tender flesh between her neck and shoulder, the spot I know always drives her crazy. "I just want to have a little sex break with my beautiful fiancée."

Two months have passed since I proposed to Brooke, and I still can't believe she's mine. Just seeing her with my ring on her finger makes me hard. I never intended on proposing to Brooke during our trip, but after seeing how well she fit in with my family and, especially, after my talk with my mother, I was ready to make her my wife. I knew it was fast at the time, but it felt right. We agreed to wait to set a date until after I'd met her dad and her brother, which was fine by me. Brooke's so close to her brother and her dad, I didn't want us doing anything without their approval first. We're going to spend the rest of our lives together, so I can wait a little longer.

"Brian, forty-five minutes of that two hours was you fucking me in the kitchen after I went to go get us more coffee." She pushes me away, denying me what I want once again.

She should know better by now than to deny me what I want. I lunge for her, pushing her back against the couch and manage to straddle her waist to keep her from escaping. Her little excited squeals are so damn cute.

"I can't help it. You look so damn sexy strutting around our apartment in these tiny shorts and this skimpy tank top that makes your tits look so damn delectable." I place a soft kiss on the top of each breast, smiling to myself when I see her nipples perk up under the thin fabric of her tank. "Brooke, I know all this stuff, backward and forward. I got this," I say confidently, dipping my head down to run my tongue along the hollow of her neck.

"Okay then, answer one last question and if you get it right, I'll let you fuck me any way you want." She flashes me a sultry grin. "What are the four distinctive facial recognition points?"

Oh yeah, she wants me to get this one right. This is the easiest question on the entire exam. "Eye color . . ." I run my lips down along her shoulder, sliding down the thin strap of her tank top, exposing her full beautiful breast. "Hair color . . ." I flick my tongue over her taut little bud, eliciting a soft moan that escapes from deep within her chest. "Recognizable scares . . ." I suck her into my warm mouth, biting down on her nipple. Her back arching off the couch. "And tattoos." I seal her lips with mine, her tongue exploring my mouth.

Brooke's hands find their way under my shirt, roaming the plains of my six pack. I break from her lips and sit up, pulling off my shirt. Needing to feel her touch over every inch of me, I'm hungry and desperate for it. She loosens her wrists from my grasp and pushes me so I'm sitting back on my knees. Her warm lips kiss down along my abs and over the whisper of hair trailing down under my belly button. Her tongue runs along my hips. My dick aches and presses against the seam of my pants.

She works open my belt and pants, looking up at me through her long lashes, licking her lips as she frees my rock hard cock. A low rumble rolls through my body when I feel her warm tongue flick over my tip, lapping up the beads of pre-cum. She gets up on her knees and pulls off her tank then wraps her tits around my hard length, working me between those big fucking breasts, and flicking her tongue along my head with each stroke down. She looks so fucking hot.

"I want to come all over those fucking tits." A low primal growl bellows out from my chest. I want nothing more than to see my cum painted all over her chest.

Her mouth returns to my cock. Licking, sucking, and kissing along my length before finally taking me into her warm wet mouth until I'm hitting the back of her throat. Just when I think she can't take me in anymore, she relaxes her throat and takes me deeper. Her mouth feels so fucking good. I fist my hand into her hair to get a better view of her fucking me with her mouth. As I run my hand along the hollow of her cheek I can feel her moans vibrating through my shaft.

"That's it Ace, make me fucking come." My hips snap against her face, feeling that familiar fire building deep inside me, and I'm ready to blow as Brooke works me like a fucking lollipop.

She pulls me out of her mouth with a pop. Her hand fisting around my cock, working up and down until I'm painting her gorgeous tits with my cum. She licks me clean then kisses the tip of my cock before sitting back on her heels. I take in the sexy view of her coated in my seed, she looks sexy as fuck.

"I love your mouth." I lean down capturing her lips with mine, tasting me on them. So fucking hot. "Thanks for helping me study, Ace."

"Well, how about you show me a little more appreciation and fuck me with this delicious cock of yours." Her dark lust filled eyes hit me right in the dick making me fucking hard again.

"With pleasure." I pull her up to her feet. Slipping my thumbs under the band of her shorts, I slide them and her panties down off her hips, letting my fingers graze along her ass. I spin her around and pull her to my chest, then press my cock between her ass cheeks. Her greedy hips grind against me. I roughly bend her over the couch, giving her ass a nice hard smack and, without warning; I grip her hips and fill her to the hilt with my dick. Her body arches back, her loud moans echo through our apartment. Fuck, her greedy pussy is clenched tighter than a fist around my length, milking my dick. "Is this what you wanted, my cock buried deep in this tight little pussy?"

"Yes! I fucking love your cock," she cries out, her hips thrusting back, meeting every hard pounding thrust.

Keeping myself firmly seated inside her slick cunt, I kneel behind her on the couch and pull her up into my arms. One hand kneading and pinching at her tits, the other reaching down between her legs, as my thumb strum rough rhythmic circles along her throbbing little bud. I can't keep my mouth from kissing and biting at her shoulder. A shudder erupts through her body and I know she's close. Her throbbing pussy urges me to come undone right along with her.

"Fuck Brooke." With one last hard snap of my hips, I'm coming, spilling every last drop into her.

I help Brooke back down onto the couch and into my arms. Softly stroking her curves as she comes down from her high, I whisper, "Thank you for helping me study, and for kicking my ass into taking the detective's exam. I never would have done this if it wasn't for you." I stared at the practice exam book for two years. The test days would come and go and I just sat and watched my brother's rise above me. Brooke gave me the kick in the ass I needed to go after my dream.

"Of course, Brian. I'm always here for you. I want you to be happy, and if being a detective makes you happy then I'm going to do everything in my power to help you live your dream. You are going to kick that test's ass tomorrow." She grabs my hand, brings it up to her lips, and places a soft kiss over each of my knuckles. "We are a team now, Brian. We are in this together. It's you and me against the world."

* * *

"Brooke baby, have you seen my dress shirt?" I call out from the bedroom, looking frantically for my uniform shirt. Today is testing day, and I'm already a bundle of nerves. I barely slept last night. My mind kept going over all the possible exam questions. It was around three in the morning when I finally passed out after waking Brooke up for a little tension relief. Now I'm exhausted on top of being stressed the fuck out.

"Ace, come on. I'm going to be late. Have you seen my shirt?" I call out again while checking under the bed.

"You mean this shirt." I look up from the floor and spot Brooke standing in the doorway of the closet wearing just my uniform shirt and a pair of dark blue cotton panties. The shirt hangs open just enough to give me a good view of the curve of her tits.

I take a hard swallow as I get up to my feet. She looks so fucking hot in my shirt and if I weren't already running late, I'd pin her against the wall and fuck her until she can't walk. I saunter to her, drinking her in. I am saving this image for later.

"This would be the one." I grin, pulling the shirt open and getting a glimpse of her full beautiful tits before sliding the shirt off and pulling it over my undershirt. "You're making it hard for me to want to leave when you look this fucking beautiful."

"Don't worry, you can . . ." She pauses, turns around, and wiggles her ass at me. I notice some pink lettering painted across her ass. I look closer and chuckle when I read what it says *Debrief me*.

"You are too damn cute, Ace." I pull her into my arms and kiss her cheek as she giggles. "When I get home tonight you better be in nothing but these panties," I order.

"Anything you want, Detective Gamble."

"A little early to be calling me Detective. I have to pass the test first." I release her from my grasp and button up my shirt. She turns around and helps me with my tie.

"You're going to ace this test and, for a little extra luck, I got you this." She unbuttons my breast front pocket, pulls out a thin card, and slips it into my hand.

I look down at the card and read the words written on the front.

"While you shield the streets, I will shield your heart."

"Turn it over." She bites her lower lip waiting for me.

I turn the card over and see that it's an ace of spades playing card with a black and white sketch of Brooke in the middle. The only color on the card is the blue in her eyes. The eyes that consumed me the moment we met. "Now you can have your lucky ace with you all the time." She looks at my face trying to gage my reaction.

"Brooke this is great, thank you."

"You're welcome. I'm glad you like it. I just wanted to do something to let you know I'm always with you, and I will always protect your heart."

This is the sweetest thing anyone's ever done for me. I can't even form the words to tell her how much I love her gesture. It means so much to me to know that, while I gave her my heart, she's still doing everything in her power to protect it.

"Brooke I love it, thank you." I pull her to my lips kissing her one last time before heading out the door. "I love you, Ace."

"I love you too, Detective."

CHAPTER THIRTY

Brooke

AFTER SHUFFLING BRIAN OUT THE door and going on my morning run with Lola, I spent the rest of the morning and afternoon distracting myself with putting the final touches on our home. I moved all my stuff over to Brian's apartment the day we came home from his cabin. He gave me free reign to decorate how I wanted. There are now photographs of the two of us hanging on the walls. And there are little touches that represent us both. Brian's name may be on the lease, but this is our home now. At least until we can find a house of our own. A place where we can start our family.

One of the first things Brian and I talked about after he proposed was having kids. Brian wants a big family with four, maybe five kids. I don't really have a number in mind. I want as many of Brian's babies as I can have.

Sitting at my desk, I feel a warm puff of air hit my leg. Lola has been passed out on my lap for most of the evening while I try to do the final read through of my book, but I keep distracting myself by staring down at my beautiful engagement ring. Brian kept his promise and found me the most perfect ring I could have ever asked for. It's an emerald cut, two-carat aquamarine diamond, set in platinum with little diamonds lining the thin band, and pretty leaf filigree wrapping around the diamond. I know I told him I didn't care about the ring but now that I have it, this all feels so real. And as soon as he meets my dad and Hunter tomorrow, we can set the wedding date, and I'll soon be Mrs. Brian Gamble. I love saying that, I even find myself writing it in my notebooks.

Mrs. Brian Gamble.

Mrs. Brooke Gamble.

Brooke Gamble.

It just sounds so damn right. I can't wait to be his wife, have his babies, and grow old together. Brian is my everything.

I've had such an uphill battle getting to this point. I've been through hell and back, and now I know it's leading me to my real happy beginning with Brian. In my heart, I know in some way Jake had a hand in guiding me here. He took control of the dart that night in his office and made it land on Seattle. He knew this was where I was supposed to be.

Coming out of la-la land, I see Lola's head perk up, signaling Brian's home.

I hear him call out for me. "Brooke baby, I'm home." Lola leaps off my lap and races out the bedroom door, barking excitedly for Brian. He walks through the doorway with Lola trotting right next to him. He's wearing my favorite sexy grin.

"Welcome home, baby." I grin, standing up from my chair and holding my arms open for him.

"I love coming home to this beautiful smiling face," he says, sliding his arms around my waist. My body instantly melts at his touch.

"How did the exam go?"

Brian's head drops down. A low sigh passes from his lips. Oh please, don't tell me he didn't pass. We spent weeks studying and preparing him for this exam. He could recite these procedures in his fucking sleep. Brian reaches behind his back, pulling something out from his back pocket. It's a white slip of paper. He slowly, almost torturously, unfolds the paper.

"I fucking passed." His loud booming excited voice carries through our entire apartment.

"Oh my God, Brian. Congratulations. I told you, you could do it," I excitedly squeal, throwing my arms around him.

"I got a perfect score. You made this happen, you gave me the strength I needed, Brooke." He lifts me up off my feet, spinning me around our bedroom.

I'm so unbelievably proud of him. He went from being on the fence about taking the exam to blowing the test and, the competition, out of the water. He's like an entirely different man from when I met him that night at his door.

"Baby, this was all you. You did this, and I'm so damn proud of you."

"I never would have if it wasn't for all your love and support." He sets me back down on my feet then cups my face in his strong hands. "I love you." He seals his lips to mine, kissing me tenderly.

"This calls for a celebration. We should go out tonight."

"I think I'd rather stay home in bed with you tonight."

"Brian come on, this is a big deal. We need to go and celebrate." I run my hands up along his chest and bat my lashes at him. "Please baby?" I lean in nice and close to his ear. "If you do this tonight, I'll let you claim my ass tonight," I offer, knowing he won't be able to say no.

Brian cocks an eyebrow up at me. "You better not be messing with me."

"I'm dead serious."

"Okay, call everyone and we'll go out." He reluctantly gives in. "But first I seem to remember telling you that you better be in those panties you wore for me this morning."

I wiggle out of his arms and turn around. Lifting up my

skirt, I let him see the *Debrief me* panties from this morning and give my ass a little wiggle for him. Brian gives me a hard slap on the ass, and Lola growls at him giving him an *I'm going to rip your throat out if you hit her again* glare.

"I don't think she thought that was funny, Daddy." I softly giggle.

Brian looks down at Lola. "I think it's time for a certain puppy to high tail her little ass out of here because Daddy is going to defile Mommy."

Lola barks at him then trots out of our bedroom and into the living room.

Brian turns back to me, a dark, hungry glint flashing in his eyes. "I think it's time for the suspect to get the debriefing of her life."

CHAPTER THIRTY-ONE

Brooke

"OH MY GOD, WILL YOU two just get a room already? Geez!" Lucy rolls her eyes at Brian and I kissing before he goes to play pool with Ryder.

"You know you don't have to watch us, Lucy. There's a thing called . . . looking away," Brian teases. He kisses my forehead, then starts walking through the crowd to join Ryder and Lucky over by the pool tables.

"God, you two are just too much."

"We're in love. And don't try and tell me you and Colton weren't the same when you were first engaged," I say taking my seat next to her at our table.

"You're right we were pretty disgustingly cute. I still can't believe you guys are getting married."

"I know . . . it's crazy. But I'm so in love with him, Lucy. I'm ready to start this next chapter of my life with him." I can't help but look over at Brian, his eyes immediately catching my gaze. Brian flashes me a wink and mouths, "I love you" to me. I blow him a kiss and mouth an, "I love you too." God, I feel like such a goofy head-over-heels in love teenager.

"I am so happy for you, sweetie. When do your dad and brother get in tomorrow?" she asks.

The day after Brian proposed, I called Hunter and my dad. My dad, of course, was worried things were moving too fast with Brian and me, but I casually reminded him that he could only wait two months after meeting my mom to marry her. After that, he kept his mouth shut on the issue. Hunter was thrilled and couldn't wait to finally meet his soon to be brother-in-law. It took some finagling with my dad's schedule to get him here the same time as Hunter's already arranged visit, but he made it happen. And I can't wait to see them both.

"They get in around noon. Brian has to work a double shift tomorrow so he can take the weekend off. So I'm going to take them around the city until Brian meets us for a late dinner."

"Well, that's sounds like fun. You should bring them by the shop. I can't wait to meet your dad and the famous Mr. Hunter." She tries to hide her smile behind her glass, but I can see it in her eyes.

Ever since Lucy saw a picture of my brother on my phone, she's had the biggest crush on him. But for her sake, she should stay as far away from Hunter as possible. I love my brother, but all he's interested in is getting a piece of ass. Lucy is too sweet and too good a friend for me to unleash my man-whore brother on. I don't want to see her get hurt.

"Oh Lord, looks like the badge bunnies are in full force tonight."

"What the hell is a badge bunny?" By Lucy's disgusted tone, it doesn't sound good.

"They're a group of girls that only like to fuck cops. And it looks like the queen bunny is making a b-line for Brian."

I look over at Brian and see a blonde in a skin tight black dress and overly teased hair walking toward him. I feel an overwhelming urge to run over there and rip her head off.

"Oh no she doesn't. Nobody touches my man." I stand up so fast my chair falls to the ground with a loud bang. I push my way through the crowd, seething mad. I've never been so pissed off and territorial before. Brian is mine and no cheap whore is ever going to lay a hand on him, unless she wants it cut off.

Just as the bimbo is about to lay her hand on Brian's shoulder, I snake in between them. Cupping Brian's face in my hands, I give him a deep passionate kiss. His hands fist in my shirt while our tongues massage against each other. Sorry Blondie, but he's mine. I break from his lips and turn to face the bunny. A shocked *what-the-fuck-just-happened* expression painted across her overly dark eye shadowed face.

"Sorry sweetheart, but he's coming home with me." I give her a half-cocked I win smirk.

"What makes you so sure?" she asks, shaking her head at me.

I lift my left hand up wiggling my fingers. "This engagement ring says he's coming home with me. So why don't you take your fake bleach blonde hair and paid for tits out of here because this guy is my man."

She rolls her eyes and starts to walk away. "Whatever! He's not even that cute anyway."

"Oh, that bitch." I start to lunge toward her, but Brian grabs me, pulling me tight against his chest.

"What the hell was that all about?"

"I saw her trying to put her hands on you, and all of the sudden I got very territorial. I don't want her touching my man." I'm still seething mad and wishing Brian would let me go so I can go teach that bitch some manners.

"That's the first time I've ever had a woman almost get in a bar fight over me. And it's fucking hot that you would rip some girl's hair out for me. But I don't want you to worry about other women, Brooke. You are the only one I want. The only one I ache for. The only one I crave. You own me Brooke, don't ever forget that."

He presses my hips tighter against him, and I can feel the growing bulge in his jeans pressing against my ass.

"This turns you on?" I ask with a chuckle.

"Just seeing you so possessive over me is kind of flattering and sexy. It shows me how much you love me." His words and his warm breath against my neck send a pleasure wave down between my legs.

"I love you so much, sometimes it's hard to breathe. Can we go home now, I really need to work off this pent up aggression." I grind my hips against him letting him know I fucking need his dick inside me.

"Fuck yeah, take it all out on me, Ace."

CHAPTER THIRTY-TWO

Brian

I WATCH BROOKE WALK BACK to the table to say goodnight to Lucy. My Brooke has one hell of a feisty side. I don't ever want her to feel jealous of another woman, because she's all the woman I will ever want or need. She's my end game. But it was pretty hot watching her become all she-bitch-from-hell over me. Made me feel even more wanted.

I scan the bar looking for Ryder so I can tell him I'm leaving. When I find him, he's in the back corner making out with some random chick in typical Ryder fashion. I pull out my phone and send him a quick text telling him I'm out of here then I head up to the bar. I wave down the bartender asking to close out my tab. Just as I finish signing the receipt I feel a cold chill course through my body as a woman slides up to the bar next to me. I don't even have to see her face to know who she is.

"That girl of yours is quite feisty." That familiar nagging voice feels like needles against my skin. Of course, now that I'm happy, she has to show her face around here again.

"What are you doing here, Jillian?" I ask, keeping my attention on the Mariners game playing on the TV hanging above the bar. She doesn't deserve my full attention.

"Oh, what, no hello for your old friend Jillian?" She reaches her hand over to my shoulder, but I pull away before she can lay so much as one finger on me.

"Let's get one thing straight Jillian, we are not now, nor will we ever be friends. Now, why don't you go crawl back into whatever dark dank hole you came from and leave me the fuck alone," I sneer, white knuckles fisting my wallet in my hand. I'd never lay a hurtful hand on a woman. I'd make an exception for Jillian.

After I found Jillian in my bed with my ex-captain, I turned and left everything I had behind, thoroughly washing my hands of her. But she still manages to haunt me, making me question myself and everyone around me. But not anymore, not now that I've found true happiness with Brooke, a woman who absolutely knows how to love.

"Does your pretty girl let you talk to her that way?"

"I don't have to because, unlike you, she knows how to treat a man." I finally turn to face her. She has a self-satisfied grin on her face, thinking she's getting under my skin. "And she knows how to keep her legs closed. Say hi to the captain for me." I turn on my heels and start walking back to Brooke.

"You're still a pathetic loser Brian, and one day your pretty girl will realize it like I did," she calls out, trying to get one last jab in.

"Jillian, you should really look at yourself in the mirror when you say shit like that."

I make it over to Brooke and grab her hand, waving goodbye to Lucy. Leading us out of the bar into the dark parking lot, I feel anger surging through my body. My mind is wild and crazed. I need a release, a release that only Brooke can give me. She's the only one that can quiet my mind.

"Brian, where are we going?"

I don't say a word just keep walking by all the cars until I come across one in the furthest darkest corner of the lot. I turn

Brooke around and roughly bend her over the hood of the car.

"I see someone can't wait until we get home." She grins at me over her shoulder as I reach under her dress and rip the thin lace of her panties clean off her body and stuff them into my pocket.

"Brooke, you know how much I love you, right?" I ask, quickly working open my pants.

"Of course, baby," she replies.

"Good, because right now I really need to fuck you like I don't." Without warning and not caring if she is ready for me, I thrust deep and hard into her tight cunt. Wrapping her hair around my fist I rear her head back hard. The sounds of our bare flesh coming together echoes through the night sky. With every hard pound, I can feel the anger and the hate fading further and further away. This is what Brooke has done for me. She's taken all my fears and anger and made them go away. She's made me a better man just by loving me.

"Oh, fuck yes, Brian," she cries out, her pussy throbbing around every inch of me. Milking me, begging me for more.

I slip a hand around her. My fingers finding her little bud swollen and desperate for attention. My thumb strums roughly over her clit. "Come for me, Brooke. I need to feel you come all over my cock."

Slowly pulling my hips back, I see her sweet juices glistening off my cock in the moonlight before I ram harder and deeper inside her. The force of each thrust pushes her further up the hood of the car. Her screams are filled with pleasure and pain as she comes. Her pussy clenches so tight around me, that it's pulling me deeper into her. I feel my orgasm building, my thrusts become wild and erratic as the surge of pleasure rips through me causing my body to shake and convulse as I spill every last drop of my seed into her. Finally, collapsing over her, I breathe hard and my mind calms as I come down from my high.

"Wow, baby. That was incredible. Where did that come from?"

I stand up, pulling out of her, and tuck myself back into my pants. I don't want to tell her about my run in with Jillian, but she's my fiancée and I can't lie to her. "I ran into Jillian while I was paying our tab."

"Oh my God. What happened, baby?" She cups my face in her hands examining my face. "Are you okay?" Her face is filled with worry.

"I'm fine now. She did what she always does which is to try and get into my head, but this time I didn't let her. I won't lie, she did piss me off, which explains what just happened, and I'm sorry for taking that out on you."

"Brian, I'm so sorry you had to go through that. But I'm not sorry for that pounding you just gave me. That was amazing. So feel free to use me for tension release anytime." She softly giggles. "She's just jealous that you have moved on and are happier now than you were with her. Don't let her get to you. You're the bigger and better person in this. So fuck her. We're about to get married and start our lives together, so focus on that," she says building me back up.

I slide my arms around her, pulling her to my lips, and kissing her softly. She always knows just the right things to say to make me feel better. And she's right, I have the love of an amazing woman, who I'm about to make my wife, and now my dream job. My life is finally heading in the right direction, and it's time I focus on that.

"I think it's time I get my beautiful fiancée home. If I remember correctly, she has some of her own pent up aggression she needs to release."

"Fuck yeah, I do. You won't be able to walk for a few days once I'm done with you."

CHAPTER THIRTY-THREE

Brooke

I PACE BACK AND FORTH along the baggage claim carousels at SeaTac Airport, fidgeting with my hands while I wait for my dad and Hunter. It's twelve-fifteen and my brother and my dad have just landed. I'm both excited and nervous about seeing them both. My stomach has been in knots all morning. My dad had reservations at first about me becoming engaged to Brian so quickly, but being his baby girl it's understandable that he would be protective. I just hope after this weekend, both him and Hunter will love Brian just as much as I do.

"Brookie," Hunter's deep, gruff voice bellows through the crowded airport.

I spin around spotting him and my dad walking toward me. Hunter's sporting a new thick beard, and his dark brown hair is a bit longer and combed back. He's dressed in his usual cargo pants and a tight fitting gray T-shirt that shows off his broad, muscular shoulders. And my dad's sporting his usual black suit and white button-up shirt.

Gee Dad, can you look any more like an FBI agent? His dark hair now showing more flecks of gray around his temples. Still the most handsome dad on the planet.

I sprint over to them, jumping into Hunter's arms and hug

him tight.

"I'm so glad you're finally here. I've missed you so much, Hunter."

He sets me back down on my feet and holds my arms out giving me a quick once over. "Seattle has done wonders for you, little sis. It's good to see you smiling again."

"Peanut, you look radiant." Dad steps past Hunter and pulls me in for a hug.

"Daddy, it's so good to see you," I say, giving him a kiss on the cheek.

"So where's the famous Brian?" my brother asks, reaching to grab his suitcase from the carousel.

"He had to work, but he's going to meet us later for dinner. Why don't we go get you two settled at the hotel, then I'll take you around to see some of the sights. A lot has changed since the last time we were all here together."

"That sounds great, Peanut. Lead the way."

⋆ ⋆ ⋆

After dropping off Hunter and my dad's luggage, I take them for a tour of the downtown area of Seattle. After lunch, I took them to some of the spots we loved when first visited the city, the waterfront where I turned every shade of red as we passed by the Ferris wheel. We walked through Pikes Place before taking them over to the Space Needle. It was the one tourist attraction we missed years ago because, at the time, Hunter was afraid of heights.

My dad is wandering around the outside viewing deck taking pictures of the incredible view of the city below us while I stand against the railing trying to focus on not throwing up my lunch. I haven't been feeling my best since this morning. My stomach has been queasy since breakfast and has proceeded to get worse as the day has gone by.

"You feeling all right, Brookie? You've turned about three shades of green since we got up here."

"I'll be fine. I think it's just the height and the swaying that are making me a little queasy. I'll be good once we get back down to earth." I give him my best fake smile even though it feels like my stomach is trying to turn itself inside out.

The elevator ride down doesn't help my current situation and, to add to my uneasy feeling, Brian hasn't been responding to any of my text messages, which is so unlike him. It's making me start to worry.

"Are you sure you're okay, Peanut? Maybe we should take you home?" My dad's tone is getting increasingly worried, as all the color drains from my face.

"I'll be fine. I just need some ginger ale to help calm my stomach."

Back down on earth some of the uneasiness goes away. We walk over to the food court at the Armory to get me some ginger ale. Standing in line, I catch Hunter winking over at one of the cashiers, a redhead in a low cut top who keeps giggling whenever Hunter looks in her direction. This little show is making me even sicker. I jab my elbow into Hunter's rib cage.

"Damn it, Brooke. What the hell?" he says huskily, rubbing his side.

"Can't you go a day without trying to nail anything with tits?"

"I could, but why would I want to," he replies, winking at the cashier again.

"You're unbelievable Hunter," I say, shaking my head in disapproval.

"Funny, that's what the flight attendant said after I landed my plane in her runway." He chuckles.

Now I really have to fight back the vomit. Typical Hunter can't keep it in his pants. When we were kids my brother made a promise to himself he would never give his heart to any woman, because he didn't want to end up like our dad. To each his own, but he could have just become a monk instead. That would be less disgusting than a giant man-whore. I just hope he doesn't try anything with Lucy when we arrive at her shop. I grab my ginger ale then pull Hunter out the door by his shirt. "Can you give me at least twenty-four hours of your time before you cross the women of Seattle off your sexual bucket list, please."

"I'm sorry Brooke. I'll be a good boy," he apologizes, as we join my dad on the monorail.

I take a seat next to my dad and rest my head on his shoulder.

"Feeling any better, Peanut?" he asks.

"A little. I think I just ate something that's not agreeing with me."

"So Brooke, the last time we talked you mentioned something about Brian starting the process of becoming a detective. How's that going?"

"He took the entrance exam yesterday and passed with flying colors. He managed to get the highest points on the test, which got him into the top five on the list for the next open spot that comes up at his precinct." I can't fight back the proud smile tugging at my lips.

"That's fantastic news. But you do realize it's going to mean longer hours at work and less time at home."

"Daddy, I am well aware of the life of being a cop. Hello! You showed me that first hand. And it doesn't bother me, Daddy. He's doing what he loves and that's what is important. If it means fewer hours a day we spend together it's okay, because we have the rest of our lives to be together."

He gives me an apologetic smile. "I'm sorry, Peanut. I just worry about you, and I want you to be happy."

I slide my hand over his, giving it a reassuring squeeze. "I am happy, Daddy. Brian makes me incredibly happy."

"Then as long as you are happy, I'm happy." He leans in and kisses the side of my head.

⋆ ⋆ ⋆

By the time we reach Lucy's shop it's hopping with the after work rush of people coming by for her array of homemade cheesecakes and pies, and a quick pick me up of espresso before heading home. Lucy spots us coming through the door and comes running from behind the counter, giving me a quick hug before greeting my brother and my dad.

"I was wondering when you all were going to get here." She turns to my dad and offers her hand to him. "It's so nice to finally meet you, Mr. McCoy. I'm Lucy Bishop."

"It's nice to finally meet the Lucy my Brooke has told us so much about. And please, call me Darrick." He shakes her hand and, before I can introduce her to Hunter, he steps in front of me and takes Lucy's hand from my dad's.

"It is an absolute honor to meet you, Lucy. I'm Hunter." He winks at her and brings her hand up to his mouth and kisses the back of her hand. I can see an excited glint in Lucy's eyes; I know she's squealing on the inside at how charming my brother is being.

"Why don't you guys take a seat, and I'll get you some coffee and pie." She starts to back up, her eyes still locked with my brother. She's so distracted by his smile she trips over a chair.

"That Lucy's a real cutie. Is she seeing anybody?" Hunter asks.

"Don't even think about it Hunter. She's too good for you, and I'm not going to let you bang my best friend then split leaving me to clean up your mess," I warn.

"She's a grown woman. A beautiful grown woman, who can make her own decisions." He looks back over at Lucy flashing her another panty-dropping smile. And I watch as her face turns a bright shade of red.

"She's a grown woman with a child, so back off." I push him into his chair.

Lucy returns a few minutes later with our coffee. I make her sit next to my dad to keep Hunter from digging his claws into her any deeper. "So how are you two enjoying Seattle so far?"

"It's a beautiful city, but not as beautiful as its charming people," Hunter chimes in, making Lucy melt into a pool on the floor. Oh, here we go again. My eyes are hurting from all the eye rolling.

"Lucy, where's Lucky? I was hoping we would see her before she headed for her shift at the club," I ask, trying to divert the conversation away from Hunter.

"She and Ryder had it out at the bar last night. Her ex, Jackson is back in town, and he stopped by the bar to see her and it set Ryder off. It's a huge damn mess."

All I knew about Jackson was that he met Lucky in San Francisco. Barely two years into dating, he broke her heart, and left her there penniless with nowhere to live. He's a real douchebag, and I can see why Ryder would be pissed about him nosing around Lucky again. Especially since I know he has feelings for her.

"I hope they can work it out."

"I hope so too. I hate it when they fight," Lucy says turning her attention back to Hunter.

We sit and continue visiting with Lucy while we sip our coffee. Hunter continues to flirt with Lucy and Lucy, of course, eats up every word of it. I'm going to have to strap a chastity belt on her and keep them separated for the rest of the time Hunter is here.

* * *

After we finish our coffee, we head back to my apartment to give my dad and Hunter a quick tour before Brian gets home from work. We round the corner and I see Brian and Ryder's cruiser parked in front of our building.

"Looks like the boys got done early," I say, as we step inside.

Strange that Brian didn't text message me that he was getting off early.

In the elevator ride up, as each floor ticks by, the rumbling in my stomach gets worse and worse. We step out of the elevator and walk down the long hallway to my apartment. I stop dead in my tracks when I see Ryder slumped down on the floor in front of our door, his head in his hands and quietly sobbing. My heart stops when I notice the blood on his hands.

"No, no, no no no," I mumble over and over stepping back away from the door.

"Brooke honey, what's wrong?" My dad tries to grab me, but I push him away.

Hunter grabs me and holds me tight as I begin to fall completely apart. Ryder hears my screams and stands up from the floor. He's white as a ghost and there's terror and panic in his eyes.

"I'm so sorry, Brooke. Brian's been shot . . ."

CHAPTER THIRTY-FOUR

Brooke

BRIAN'S BEEN SHOT.

Brian's . . . been . . . shot.

Every word, every syllable of Ryder's words cut through me like a hot knife.

This isn't happening.

This can't be happening.

This has to be a nightmare. Please, God, let this be a nightmare.

Come on Brooke, wake up, you're dreaming. Please just wake up. But no, I'm awake and this is actually happening. This pain I'm feeling is real, and all I want to do is curl up and die.

I'm sobbing uncontrollably into Hunter's chest while my dad tries to get the details of what happened from Ryder. I can only hear about every other sentence. Something about a meth lab bust gone wrong. A few other officers were also caught in the line of fire, but mainly just minor gunshot wounds. Brian's in the worst shape.

"Brooke, I'm so sorry, I got distracted and didn't see which room Brian went into. This is all my fault." His voice is laced with regret and pain and the tears are streaming down his face. At this point, I couldn't care less how sorry he is.

"You got distracted." I turn to face him. My entire body is searing hot with anger. "You're a cop Ryder, you're supposed to be focused with a clear head at all times. You're his best friend, his partner, his brother. You're supposed to have his back." I back him up against the door. "You're supposed to protect him, protect each other. You let him down, you let me down. How could you let this happen?" I start beating my fists against his chest, screaming, "It should've been you. It should've been you."

Hunter grabs me and pulls me away from Ryder. I try lunging for him again, but he wraps me tighter in his arms. My dad stands between Ryder and me. Ryder is mumbling and sobbing, "I'm sorry," over and over again. I don't care, he let his guard down and now my fiancé is lying in a hospital fighting for his life.

"Brooke, calm down. Screaming at Ryder is not going to help anyone," Dad shouts then turns his attention to Ryder. "What hospital did they take him to?"

"University of Washington Hospital," he mumbles.

"Until Brooke calms down, I think it's best you go see if the precinct has made arrangements to send a patrol team to pick up his mother and sister to bring them to the hospital. Hunter and I will take Brooke over to the hospital." He rests a comforting hand on Ryder's shoulder. "Look, you made a mistake, it happens to the best of us, but right now you need to focus and man up and show your partner you care by getting his family to that hospital."

"Yes, sir." Ryder mouths another "I'm sorry" then bolts for the emergency stairwell.

⋆ ⋆ ⋆

The car ride to the hospital is so quiet you could hear a pin drop. I sit in the back with Hunter seated next to me while my dad drives. Hunter holds my hand the entire time. All I can do is stare out the window watching the world move in slow motion. Time seems to stand still from the moment I heard Ryder tell me Brian had been shot. Brian is my world, and now my world is slipping away from me again.

When we pull up to the hospital parking lot, Hunter helps me out of the car. My dad and Hunter each wrap an arm around me and escort me into the emergency room. The moment we step through the sliding doors we're met by a sea of police officers.

"What are they all doing here?" I whisper to my dad.

"They are here for Brian, sweetheart," he replies. "This is what we do for a fallen brother."

The crowd begins to part as we walk further inside, each officer giving me a warm, sympathetic smile as we pass. Brian really must mean a lot to these men and women for them to all drop everything to come show him support. Once we reach the nurses station we're met by Brian's Captain.

"Miss McCoy, I'm Captain Pierce with the Second Precinct. Just wanted to let you know on behalf of all of us from the Second that we're here for you and whatever you might need."

"Thank you Captain Pierce, all I really want to know is how is Brian, is there any word on his condition?" I take a deep breath, trying to prepare myself for the worst.

"He took three GSW's to the vest, one of which ripped through and into his right shoulder. Another bullet hit him in the side piercing his liver." I squeeze Hunter's arm tighter as the tears begin to fall again from my eyes. "He also suffered a concussion, broken ribs, and a broken leg from his fall out the window. The doctors have him up in surgery now and they'll come see you once they have any more news." He gives me a sympathetic smile then escorts us up to the surgical floor waiting room.

CHAPTER THIRTY-FIVE

Brooke

IT'S MIDNIGHT, THE HALLS OF the hospital are eerily quiet except for the faint sounds of beeping machines. I had to get away and breathe or at least try to. I couldn't take another minute of sitting in that waiting room with everyone's sad faces staring at me. I couldn't take seeing the sadness and pain in Brian's mother's face. First she loses her husband to this job and now she might be losing her son. It was killing me.

We hadn't heard much from the surgical team other than they were doing everything in their power to keep Brian alive. Just two days ago, we were so happy, so in love, like a couple of giddy teenagers who couldn't keep their hands off of each other. Who loved each other with such intensity that it could fuel the sun. We were ready to start our lives together, but now I'm in another hospital about to lose the man I love most in this world for the second time.

I pass by the dark cafeteria and stumble upon the hospital chapel. It's quiet and empty and the only light in the room is from a few flickering candles. I must be desperate because I cross the threshold. Walking up to the small altar, I grab one of the matchsticks and light a candle using the flame of another candle, and then I take a seat in the front pew.

I haven't stepped inside a church since my mother's funeral. After I spent every day while she was sick in a chapel like this one in a hospital in Boston, praying and begging God not to take my mom, I lost my faith when my prayers went unanswered and she passed way. Since then God and I haven't been on the best of terms.

But now I'm desperate. Desperate enough to come back to God to beg him not to take another person I love from me.

I stare up at the crucifix hanging on the wall above the altar and start to speak, "Hi. I know it's been a while since you've seen me in one of your houses, and I know we haven't been on the best of terms, but I'm desperate. I know you have a plan for everyone, and I just want to know what I did to deserve this shitty road you've put me on? What did I do to deserve having everyone I care so much for ripped from me? First my mom, then Jake, and now you're trying to take Brian from me." I suck in a sharp breath as the tears begin to flow again.

"When you took Jake from me it almost destroyed me. But if you take Brian it will kill me. I won't survive losing him, he's everything to me. I can't breathe without him. Please don't take him from me . . . please? I can't live without him." I sit in this quiet chapel sobbing and quietly pleading with God and anyone who can hear me. Just then I hear Hunter's voice behind me.

"Brooke, Brian's out of surgery."

⋆ ⋆ ⋆

Hunter and I race back upstairs to surgery. The doctors have taken Brian's mom and sister back to see him. I run straight for the nurse's station and pound on the counter to get the nurse's attention. She looks up from her computer screen flashing me an annoyed glare.

"What's the status on Brian Gamble?"

"And you are?" she asks looking up at me over the rim of her glasses.

"I'm his fiancée. Please, can you tell me if he's going to be okay?"

She picks up Brian's chart and starts reading the doctor's notes. They were able to repair the damage to his liver and arm. There was no bleeding or brain injuries from the grade three concussion he suffered.

I collapse into Hunter's arms when I hear her say the words, "After some rehabilitation he will make a full recovery."

"Can I see him?" I ask, feeling a huge sense of relief wash over me.

"I will take you back to see him." She gives me a warm, comforting smile as she stands up from her desk.

We walk down the quiet corridor and as we get closer to Brian's room, I can hear his mother crying. I pause to give Eliana and Natalie a hug making sure they're okay. The nurse steps inside Brian's room first and pushes back the curtain. The moment I see Brian lying on his bed hooked up to machines and tubes and with wires hanging off him, it sends a haunting chill through my body. I hesitate at first, not having the strength to move my feet. I feel a force pulling me, urging me to go inside. I step over the threshold and walk to the foot of his bed, and bring my hand up to my mouth as I look down at his lifeless body.

"He is still under anesthesia, so he could be out for a while. He isn't completely out of the woods yet. There is still a chance of infection and possible internal bleeding due to his pierced liver. He will need to be monitored closely for the next few days, and he will also need physical therapy for his broken leg and injured shoulder." The nurse slides one of the chairs over to the left side of his bed for me. "The best thing that you can do for him right now is talk to him. Give him a reason to fight." She leaves the room and tends to Brian's mom and sister outside. I take a deep breath then walk over to the chair, taking my seat.

She said to give him a reason to fight, I have a pretty damn good reason for him.

I slip my hand into his, being careful not to disturb the IV in his hand. Gently, I rub my thumb along his warm skin. The sound of the monitors beeping make it hard to think.

"Brian it's me, your lucky ace." My voice is shaky and scared. "Brian, I really need you to fight. I don't think I can do all this on my own. You're my light, Brian. My savior. Before you I was lost and drowning and you saved me. You gave me a home and a reason to live. Without you I am lost."

I bend down and kiss the top of his hand. "Don't give up on us, Brian. Please baby just fight. I can't do this without you. I can't raise our baby without you."

CHAPTER THIRTY-SIX

Brian

"FIGHT FOR US . . . our baby." The words echo through my mind as I struggle to open my eyes. I try to call out for Brooke to tell her I'm here, but the words just won't come out. My head is pounding in my ears and, every time I breathe in, I can feel a searing pain rip through my chest. Then I hear the sweetest sound on earth.

"Oh my god, Brian. Brian baby, I'm here." I can feel her warmth radiating next to me. The touch of her hand to mine sets my body alive, and my urgency to see her only fuels my need to get my eyes open.

Brooke calls out for the nurse and the doctor. I try to talk, try to call out to Brooke but the words still won't come out. My throat is raw and aches. A bright beam of light shines in my eyes blinding me even more from seeing my girl. All I want is to see her face . . . to know I really am alive.

My eyes finally start to come into focus, and I see Brooke standing with her back to me talking to the doctor.

I hear a muffled, "He's going to make a full recovery" come from the doctor.

Brooke gives him a grateful hug and thanks him repeatedly. Come on baby turn around, I need to see you.

"Brooke," I manage to rasp out. Brooke turns around and the way the light from the window glows around her makes her look like an angel.

"Brian, I'm here." Her warm smile and the touch of her hand on my cheek makes me forget all about the pain.

"Brooke." I reach my hand up, cupping her cheek. She's real. I'm not dreaming.

"It's me, Brian." She pours me a cup of water and helps put the straw in my mouth. The cool water soothes the burning in my throat from the breathing tube. "Do you remember what happen?"

"I remember getting the call to an abandoned factory to investigate a potential meth lab. Ryder and I were sent to help clear the building. We were up on the last floor when a guy came out of nowhere guns-a-blazing. I felt the first bullet rip through my vest, then next thing I know I'm on the ground outside the building with paramedics all around me." I take another sip of water. I can't keep my eyes off Brooke, I've missed her face. "How long have I been out?" It feels like I've been asleep for a year.

"Just for a day or so. You gave us a big scare, Brian." The tears begin to well up in her eyes. "I don't know what I would've done if I lost you." It breaks my heart to know how much pain and worry I've put her through.

"Hey, no. Come here, Brooke." I tug on her hand in a way that gives her no other choice but to climb into bed with me. She carefully lies next to me, wrapping my arm around her. God, it feels good to hold her again. "Brooke, I will always come back to you. I will fight heaven and hell, nothing will ever keep me from you. It was hearing your words urging and begging me to keep fighting that kept me going, kept me fighting to get back to my girl."

Then I remember the other thing that made me fight even

harder, the words "our baby" kept repeating over and over in my mind. Was Brooke really pregnant? I needed to know.

"Brooke, I heard everything you said to me while I was unconscious." I feel her body stiffen, her breathing becoming deep and nervous. "Brooke, are you pregnant?"

"Yes." She looks away from me, trying to hide the tears now streaming down her cheeks. I know she's scared because we wanted to wait until after we were married and after I was officially made detective, but I don't care, this baby's meant to be here with us.

"When did you find out?"

"The night you were shot. I was walking around the hospital trying to keep myself distracted while we waited to hear from the doctor. Eventually I made my way up to the nursery. I looked at the little babies in their bassinets and it dawned on me why I haven't been feeling well . . . that I might be pregnant. I asked one of the nurses if she could give me a pregnancy test and it came back positive. I'm so sorry, Brian. I thought we were so careful." She sniffles wiping her tear-stained cheeks.

I place my hand over her stomach. We're having a baby, I can barely wrap my mind around the idea. I had always wanted a family, but after everything that had happened with Jillian; I buried that hope away with what was left of my heart. It wasn't until I met Brooke that I started thinking about kids again, and now it's actually happening, my dream is finally coming true.

If I could move, I'd leap out of this bed and run down the halls screaming that I'm going to be a father.

"Brooke, you're making my dream come true, you don't have anything to be sorry for."

"You're really happy about this?" she asks shyly.

"Happy doesn't even begin to describe how I'm feeling right now. I know we didn't plan for this to happen, but this baby is a blessing." I give her a reassuring smile. "Brooke, you and this baby are my everything. Everything I am and everything I have is for the two of you. I love you so much."

"I love you too, Brian." She leans in pressing her lips against mine, kissing me gently.

I don't care how painful this is going to be, I can't fight back my excitement anymore, I break from her lips and shout at the top of my lungs, "We're having a baby!"

CHAPTER THIRTY-SEVEN

Brooke

Six Months Later

"LUCY, CAN YOU COME HELP zip me up?" I call out from my room.

"Of course, sweetheart." Lucy replies, stopping in her tracks when she enters the room seeing me in my wedding dress for the first time.

It's my wedding day, a day six months ago when Brian was fighting for his life in that hospital bed, I thought would never come. But now, here I am in my perfect wedding dress, carrying Brian's baby, and ready to become his wife. My heart feels so full of love it could burst. I've been counting down the days, hours, and minutes since Brian and I set the date. Brian was still in the hospital recuperating when we agreed that we wanted to get married before our little bundle of joy came into this world. So we set the date for when we knew Brian's injuries would be healed enough he could stand up at the altar.

Lucy and Brian's sister, Natalie, and his mother all helped me with planning the wedding, even filling in meetings for me with caterers and the florist when I was too sick with morning sickness. They have been an absolute godsend. Lucy graciously volunteered her house for the ceremony and reception as all the good reception spaces were booked. She has a beautiful home with a gorgeous view of Lake Washington from her backyard, which is currently blooming with fall roses, Iceland poppies, pansies, and snapdragons. We set up a tent and heaters on the back patio to accommodate all of our guests and keep them safe from the fall rains.

"My God, Brooke, you look so beautiful." She steps up behind me and slowly zips up the bodice of my dress, then carefully does up each of the tiny buttons. "Brooke, I take back everything I said about you getting this dress. You're going to take Brian's breath away when he sees you." Her face is beaming at me through the mirror.

I fell in love with my dress the moment I saw it in the bridal shop. It's a long, white, strapless silk taffeta trumpet style gown that hugs my curves and my baby bump perfectly. It also has a row of buttons that go all the way down the back to the long train. To complete my look, I've left my hair down in loose curls, and I'm wearing a tiara of orange and pink wildflowers from Lucy's garden. Lucy thought I was crazy for getting a dress that shows off my pregnant belly, but I didn't care, I want our family and friends to know how proud I am to be carrying Brian's baby girl.

A girl.

A little girl that will be a perfect mix of Brian and me. Before we found out the sex of the baby, Brian was so sure it was going to be a boy, even to the point of going out and buying a tiny baseball mitt. I thought for sure he was going to be upset when the doctor said girl, but in true sweet Gamble style he said he couldn't wait to teach his little girl how to play catch. We decided to name her Ella, after my mom to honor her memory. I still believe in my heart that my mom, Jake, and Brian's dad were in heaven working together to make this day happen.

"So are you nervous at all?" Lucy asks, adjusting my crown

of flowers.

"Surprisingly no. I'm more anxious to get down the aisle to marry Brian." Through this whole planning process, I haven't been nervous or stressed at all. This feels right, so what's there to be nervous about.

Lucy gives me one last look in the mirror and the water works start immediately as she slips her arms around me. "I am so happy for you, Brooke. You and Brian deserve all the happiness in the world."

"Thank you, Lucy. Thank you for everything. You've been the best maid of honor a girl could ever ask for." I rest my head against hers. "I just wish Lucky was here."

We both let out a sad sigh, missing our girl. During my bachelorette party, Brian, Ryder, and the rest of their crew showed up at Lucky's club. It was a memorable night in more ways than one. Brian and Ryder both gave me a drunken lap dance. It was also the first night in months that Ryder and I laughed and had fun together again. After Brian got shot it took weeks for me to even look Ryder in the face. He let his emotions over fighting with Lucky the night before distract him from his job. Brian convinced me that it was an accident. An accident that would live with Ryder for the rest of his life, and if I didn't forgive him it would only eat away at him even worse. I know what it's like to have that kind of pain eat away at you and I didn't want Ryder feeling that way for the rest of his life, so I forgave him. Now we are getting back to where we were before the shooting.

At some point in the evening, Ryder and Lucky had disappeared. We all thought it was to make amends after the fight they had a few months earlier after Jackson, Lucky's ex, had shown back up. The next day she left Lucy and me a text message saying she was sorry, but she needed to get away. We haven't heard from her since. Ryder is no help, he refuses to divulge any details of what actually happened that night, but instead has decided to use booze and girls as a way to cope with her being gone. I miss her so much and wish she would just come home already.

"I know, I wish she was here too, but we have more important things to worry about, starting with getting you down to see your groom to be." Lucy hands me my bouquet of orange and red roses then grabs the hem of my train and follows me downstairs to see Brian before the ceremony.

I wanted Brian and I to have a private moment together that was just for us before the craziness of the day crept in.

As soon as I walk into the living room, Ella starts kicking me like crazy. She always knows when Brian is near. Such a daddy's girl already. She's definitely going to have Brian completely wrapped around her finger the moment she arrives. I step further inside the quiet room and see Brian standing with his back to me by the wall of windows that overlook the backyard. Lucy gives me a quick kiss on the cheek then leaves us in private.

I take a few steps closer to Brian, taking a moment to drink him in, in his dark blue suit. He catches my reflection in the glass and turns around. His big brown eyes widen with excitement, and the tears start to well as he gazes upon me.

"Brooke." My name comes out in a whispered hush.

"Don't start with the tears now," I warn feeling my own tears beginning to build.

He looks so handsome in his suit with his hair neatly combed back and his newly grown beard. I love that he let his beard grow out, he looks so damn handsome with it, and it feels so good against my skin. I'm definitely looking forward to beard burn all over my body during our honeymoon.

"I'm sorry, Ace, but you look so beautiful." He pauses in front of me, then dips his head down to give me a gentle kiss on the lips.

"You better say hello to little Miss Ella, she's been kicking like crazy since I stepped in here." I smile, pointing to my bump just as Ella kicks me again.

"I would never forget her." Brian takes a step back then leans down placing his hands on my belly and kisses my bump. "I love you, Ella." Ella responds with a mighty kick as if saying, *I love you too*. "I think we're going to have a little soccer player on our hands." Brian chuckles standing back up.

"She was playing quite the game last night. I swear she knows when you aren't around, and last night she knew Daddy wasn't in bed with Mommy. She's such a daddy's girl."

"I missed you both last night too. Don't worry Ella, Daddy will always be here for you and Mommy." He leans down and gives my bump another kiss. "So, Miss McCoy, are you ready to be my wife?" he asks as he brings my left hand up to his mouth and kisses my ring finger.

"I've been ready for this day since you kissed me in the elevator."

"You mean the day you raped my mouth after you called me . . . What was it again? Oh yeah, a pathetic waste of space." He laughs.

"Those were my exact words. You were the one that was all up in my bubble, taunting me with those delicious lips of yours. How was a girl to resist?" We both laugh, and Brian pulls me into his arms and rains kisses down my face and neck. His beard tickles my skin.

"I fucking love you," he mumbles between kisses.

"I love you too."

Brian starts to lean in for another kiss, but his mom interrupts, letting us know that they are ready to begin the ceremony. Brian gives me one last quick kiss. "I'll meet you at the end of the aisle."

I watch Brian walk out to the tent. I can't wait to marry this man.

Eliana joins me in the living room. "Brooke you look exquisite, sweetheart." She pulls me in for a hug. "I'm so happy to welcome you into our family, and I especially can't wait for this sweet girl to join us, too." She softly smiles cradling my bump in her hands.

Eliana has been so great through this whole process. One thing I missed most about planning the wedding was that my mom wasn't here to be a part of it. But Eliana filled in and made me feel like her daughter. She will never know how much that means to me.

"I have *a little something old* for you." She opens a small black box and pulls out a small gold heart shaped locket with a G inscribed on the front. "This locket was given to me by my mother when I married Brian's father. This was never Natalie's style, so I held onto it in case Brian finally did get married. Inside, I put a picture of you and Brian, then when little Ella comes you can put a picture of her in it."

"Eliana, this is so sweet of you. Thank you so much. I love it." I lift my hair up so she can do up the clasp.

"It looks perfect on you. Okay, I better get out there. Welcome to the family, sweetheart." Eliana steps outside and joins the rest of the wedding party out by the tent.

"Brookie, wow!" I hear Hunter call out as he walks down the stairs with my dad, and they are both rendered speechless for the moment.

"Peanut, you look beautiful. You're positively glowing."

"Thanks, Daddy. So are you boys ready to give me away?" I smile, giving them both a hug.

"I don't think either one of us is ready." Hunter wipes a tear from his eye.

"Hey Hunter, don't cry. I'm always going to be your Brookie, that's never going to change. I love you big brother and thank you for everything you've done for me." Hunter pulls me into his arms giving me as big a hug as he can with my protruding belly.

I always knew when I got married I wanted both my dad and Hunter to give me away. They've both been there for me through everything, and Hunter has gone from just being my older brother to being like a second father to me. He has more than earned this right.

"Brooke, I know your mother is looking down on you today, and I know she is so proud of the woman you have become. I am so proud of you too, Brooke."

Damn it, I didn't want to cry, but here we are two grown ass men and me, hugging together in a crying mess.

Lucy pokes her head through the door and tells us it's time, and my heart flutters with excitement.

"Ready or not, it's time." I slide an arm through each of theirs. We step outside into the cool fall night. The air is thick with the smell of rain and fresh flowers. As we wait outside the marquee, I stand on my tiptoes to get a glimpse inside. The small marquee is glowing with candles and filled with every flower from Lucy's garden . . . and half the florists in Seattle. Lucy went a little overboard with helping pick out the flowers, but it looks absolutely beautiful.

The music begins and my dad looks over at me. "Are you ready?"

"I'm ready."

CHAPTER THIRTY-EIGHT

Brian

STANDING AT THE END OF the altar, I anxiously await Brooke. This day had been a long time coming. We've been through hell and back to get to this day, but I wouldn't change a minute of it, because, today, I'm marrying my best friend.

The music begins and our guests rise the moment Brooke steps inside the tent. My beautiful Brooke looks like a vision coming down the aisle toward me. Her face beaming in the candle light. I'm one lucky son of a bitch. This incredible woman chose *me* to spend the rest of her life with.

Once they reach the altar, Derrick shakes my hand then pulls me into a hug and whispers, "Take care of my little girl." He has nothing to worry about, I'm going to spend the rest of my life treating Brooke like a queen. Derrick takes Brooke's hand from his and places it in mine. Hunter reluctantly lets Brooke's arm go and walks over to me to shake my hand.

"Welcome to the family, Brian. Please take care of my sister, she's all I have." I know this is hard for both Derrick and Hunter to give Brooke away. It seems to be hitting Hunter even harder. He's been there for her through some of the best and worst times in her life. They have a special bond and I will never come between that.

"You have nothing to worry about. I'm going to take really good care of Brooke."

Hunter gives Brooke a kiss on the cheek then joins his father at the edge of the alter.

Brooke and I step up to the altar and I whisper a quick, "I love you" to Brooke before she turns to hand her bouquet to Lucy. We join hands. The minister begins the ceremony with his speech, and the world around us just fades away. It's just Brooke and me, looking lovingly into each other's eyes.

Before I know it, I hear the minister say it's time for us to exchange our vows, and my heart begins to beat a little quicker and my nerves try to set in, but I simply focus on Brooke and block out the rest of the world.

"A year ago, almost to the day, a mouthy brunette with the biggest blue eyes I'd ever seen came knocking on my door to complain about the noise. I won't go into the details of what said noise was, but she was pretty teed off." Brooke chuckles softly. "I didn't know it at the time, but that was the day I met the woman I was going to marry. Before I met you, I was wandering lost in the darkness and, like a bright beam of light, you pulled me out of the hell I'd been living in. You've made me a better man by simply loving me for all that I am. You are the love of my life, and I promise I will spend every day, for the rest of my days, making you and our baby as happy as you have made me."

Brooke reaches up and gently wipes my tears away and whispers, "I love you" before starting her vows.

"I've heard people say how happy they are that we have found our happy ending, but I don't like to think of it that way. This isn't our ending, this is our beginning, because our story is nowhere near the end. We have a new chapter ahead of us. Though we don't know what awaits us, I know as long as we have each other and the love that burns between us, we can get through anything." She pauses to take a calming breath. "Brian, I have fallen more in love with you each passing day we are together, and I know that our love is only going to grow even bigger as we continue our lives together. I am so proud and honored that you chose me to be your wife, and the mother of your child. I love you so much."

After she's finished, I can't help but steal a quick kiss before we exchange rings.

The minister finally says the words that I've been dying to hear.

"It's with great pleasure that I announce for the first time, Mr. and Mrs. Brian Gamble."

I fucking love the way that sounds.

Our guests stand to clap and cheer for us.

I lift our hands in the air and shout, "We're fucking married!"

* * *

The cake's been cut and the speeches have been given. The party's beginning to die down. Ryder and Lucy are drunk and singing eighties rock ballads with the band, while my nieces dance in circles on the dance floor with Bailey and my sister. The wedding's gone off without a hitch, I couldn't have asked for a more perfect day.

Brooke and I make our final rounds around the party saying our goodbyes. I can't wait to get Brooke alone and give her the surprise I've been keeping for the past two months. I help Brooke into the limo then give the driver the address to the real location where we'll be spending our first night as man and wife.

"I can't wait to get you back to the hotel and out of this suit." Brooke leans over kissing down my neck.

"You won't have to wait until we get back to the hotel."

The limo pulls up to a house just four houses down from

Lucy's. "We're here."

Brooke gives me a confused look. "Where are we? I thought we were going to the hotel?"

The driver opens Brooke's door and helps her out. I follow behind and grab her hand leading her up the walkway to the two-story white house with black shutters and the red door. Brooke mentioned months ago how much she loved this house and how perfect it would be for our family. Then about a week after she pointed it out to me for the fifth time, it went on the market, so I bought it.

"Brian seriously, what are we doing here?" she asks again.

We reach the door and I pause reaching into my suit pocket. I pull out a small silver key and hand it to her. "Welcome home, Mrs. Gamble."

She stares down at the key in her hand, her other hand is over her mouth as she quietly cries, "You bought us a house? Brian, when did you do this?"

"About two months ago. Lucy called me the day she saw the 'for sale' sign out front. I knew how much you loved this house, so I called that day and made an offer. Come on, let's go see our new home."

CHAPTER THIRTY-NINE

Brooke

I PUSH THE KEY INTO the deadbolt and open the door. Before I can take a step, Brian lifts me up in his arms and carries me over the threshold. The house is dark except for a trail of tea light candles and rose petals leading upstairs. Brian sets me back down on my feet, and I step further into the house. I take a moment to look around the empty space, my mind already picturing warm fires in the fireplace. Pictures of our family on the walls, and Ella and Lola playing on the floor in the living room while I cook dinner in my new kitchen.

"Do you like it?" Brian asks. He's just standing in the doorway of the living room watching me.

"Brian, I love it. I can't believe you bought us a house." I can't believe he managed to keep it a secret for so long. I'm even more surprised Lucy was able to keep her big mouth shut.

"I wanted us to have a fresh start in a place that we could make ours. A proper home for Ella and any future children to grow up in. Plus, it's close to Lucy so she can come help out with Ella when I'm at work. Come on, I want to show you something."

He leads me upstairs to one of the four bedrooms. Hanging in the middle of the white painted door is a little plaque with

Ella written in pink lettering. He opens the door and turns on the light, revealing Ella's fully decorated nursery. And now it all comes flooding back to me. While Lucy was helping me with some last minute wedding stuff, she brought out all these baby magazines and kept asking me which nurseries I thought were cute. I didn't think anything of it at the time and just forgot about it. I step inside and see everything I had pointed out, the white sleigh style crib, the crystal chandelier with the little crystal butterflies, and the mint green rocker that reminded me of the one my mom had when I was a baby.

"Brian, I can't believe you did this."

"Lucy is the one you should be thanking for all of this."

I run my hands along the crib. Glancing up at the little shelf hanging on the wall, mixed in with the pictures of me and Brian, is a picture of my mom holding me in my old bedroom when I was a baby. And with that the tears begin to fall again. I grab the picture and run my fingers along the glass. Brian comes up behind me and wraps his arms around me.

"Your dad found that in some old boxes and sent it to Lucy knowing you'd want it. It's kind of like she will be here watching over Ella."

Just when I think I can't possibly love Brian more, he goes and does something like this that makes me fall even harder in love with him. I love this man with every ounce of my being, he consumes every part of me. He is forever etched into my soul. I can't wait for the journey that is ahead of us.

* * *

Brian

As we quietly stand in Ella's room, I can't help but think back over the past year and the roller coaster ride that brought us to this moment. Our hatred . . . turning into an intense love for each other . . . to me almost dying. But I wouldn't change a second of it, because it brought me Brooke and very soon our beautiful daughter.

Love is the ultimate gamble and there are always risks, but when you love someone as much as I love Brooke, the gamble is always worth the risks.

EPILOGUE

Brian

BROOKE IS FRANTICALLY SEARCHING THROUGH her closet for something to wear to her book signing while I'm in bed with Ella blowing raspberries on her tiny belly. Her sweet little giggles and squeals fill the room. I can't believe how quickly she is growing. Seems like yesterday we were bringing her home from the hospital and now she's crawling around. She is such a happy baby. Always has a smile on her face. She has Brooke's big blue eyes and my nose. She's a perfect combination of the two of us.

"Are you sure you don't want me to call Lucy or Natalie to come watch Ella?" Brooke calls out from the closet.

"Brooke come on, I'll be fine. She's my kid, it's my job to take care of her," I reply then look back at Ella and mouth, "mommy's crazy" before blowing on her belly again.

"I know but you've never taken care of Ella on your own for an entire day before. Maybe I should just call my publicist and have her reschedule the book signing for next week when your mom is feeling better."

I scoop up Ella and head into the closet where I find Brooke half zipped in her dress with two different shoes on. She is looking in the mirror trying to decide which shoe goes with her dress. "You are not rescheduling. Your adoring public is waiting for you. Ella and I will be fine. I have all your notes, and I'm the king of diaper changes. I got this." I flash her a reassuring smile, trying to hide the fact that I'm really freaking out on the inside. Sure, I've taken care of Ella while Brooke napped or went out for a couple hours with Lucy or my mom, but this is the first time it will be me own all day with Ella. To say I'm nervous is an understatement.

"Okay. I should be back by six, and I will stop and pick up your favorite pizza for dinner, then later, after Ella goes to bed, I will take care of daddy." Brooke grins, leaning in giving me a kiss.

"Daddy likes the sound of that." I smirk kissing her again. "P.S. Wear the black spiky ones," I say, leaning in close to her ear. "Make sure those are the only thing you are wearing tonight after Ella goes to bed." I can see her body shudder at my statement. I love the effect I have on her.

"Mmmmm whatever daddy wants." She flashes a sultry grin before turning around to have me help zip up her dress. She switches her shoes and I can't help but picture those spiky heels digging into my back later tonight.

"Be a good girl for daddy, Ella. I love you both." She gives Ella a kiss on her little chubby cheek then gives me one last kiss goodbye before heading out for her book signing.

I look down at Ella and the big slobbery grin on her face. "First, we are taking off this crazy thing." I chuckle. Pulling off the big white and black polka dot bow head band off her head. "Now what do I do, because daddy has no fucking clue what he's doing. See? I'm already messing up; I just dropped the f-bomb in front of you." I am totally screwed.

Ella looks up at me and sticks her tongue out, blowing a raspberry at me and giggles.

"Thanks for that vote of confidence, kid."

* * *

Ella kept me on my toes for most of the morning. First, she pee'd all over the changing table while I changed her diaper, then proceeded to get into everything that wasn't locked or nailed down. Even crawling out the dog door while I was fixing her bottle. After about ten minutes of searching the house I finally found her out by Lola's dog house, chewing on Lola's chew toys while Lola chewed on Ella's teething ring. The father of the year award goes to . . .

I finally wrangle Ella back into the house. I plop us down on the floor in the living room and I pull out a blue plastic box with a police shield on the front from the toy bin. Inside the box are plastic toy versions of the gear that I carry while on duty. Ella immediately grabs the plastic set of handcuffs and brings them to her mouth then proceeds to chew on them.

"Of course you would go for the handcuffs first. You're just like mommy. But that's a tale you will never hear, because as far as these are concerned, they are only for locking up very bad people, and if anyone tells you otherwise I will beat them to death with my night stick," I warn. I can almost hear Brooke in my head saying, "But I've been a very bad girl, Detective Gamble." Fucking love my dirty woman.

I reach into the box and pull out the blue and silver plastic taser, holding it out to Ella.

"Now, your taser only makes noises, but daddy's, on the other hand, will give any guy that lays a hand on you a taste of what five thousand volts of electricity feels like. And daddy's a cop so he can make it look like an accident." If Ella grows up to be half as beautiful as Brooke, we will have our hands full. But if I had it my way she won't date until I'm dead in the ground.

While Ella plays with her toys I collapse back onto the floor, feeling completely exhausted. It's only one in the afternoon and

I already feel like I've worked a double shift at the precinct. I can't believe one tiny infant could be so much work. Brooke makes it look so easy. I don't know how she does this every day. I have a whole new respect for what she does around here.

"Da Da," Ella coos as she crawls over to me. She sweetly smiles at me and then gives me a big slobbery kiss on the lips.

"Aww thanks, monkey." I smile, scooping her up into my arms and holding her above me. I make silly faces at her while she giggles uncontrollably. It's the sweetest sound on earth. Bringing her down to my lips, I place a kiss on her cheek. I hold her while I carefully stand back on me feet. "I think it's lunch time. Let's go see what mommy left for us to eat."

I buckle Ella in her high chair then set to work making lunch for us. "Well kid, looks like you get smushed bananas and carrots, yum. And daddy gets leftover pastrami on rye." I set Ella's plate down on her tray and take a bite of my sandwich before taking my seat in front of her.

The bananas go down with ease. The carrots, on the other hand, take a little more convincing on my part. I place the spoon in my mouth, downing the bite of the cold mushy carrots, trying to hide the look of disgust on my face as I swallow them down. Ella giggles then reluctantly takes a few more spoonfuls of her lunch.

I clean up the lunch dishes then pick up Ella out of her high chair just in time for her to spit up her lunch all over herself and me. "Perfect." I let out a frustrated sigh. I escort us both upstairs to the bathroom. I carefully peel off our food crusted clothes then turned on the shower, checking the temperature before stepping inside with Ella. While rinsing off Ella, she lets out a big yawn as her busy morning of play catches up with her. "Looks like we are both ready for a nap," I say, letting my own yawn escape my lips.

I finish rinsing us both off, and I wrap Ella up in a big fluffy towel, then wrap one around my waist. I dress Ella in one of her white onesies, and dress myself in a pair of flannel pajama pants and a T-shirt. I make Ella a bottle then carry her back up to her room. Taking a seat in the rocking chair, I rock back and forth gently as she drinks her bottle. She stares up at me while I sing to her softly, just like Brooke does. She looks at me with such love in her eyes and it's moments like this that make me feel so damn thankful and blessed to have Brooke and now Ella in my life. These two are my absolute world and nothing else matters as long as I have them.

Ella is peacefully asleep snuggled against my chest as I walk us back to our bedroom. She looked so sweet I couldn't bring myself to put her down in her crib. Instead, I bring her into our bed with me to nap. This precious little girl has me completely wrapped around her tiny fingers, and I'm loving every minute of it.

* * *

Brooke

The house is completely dark when I pull up just after six. My book signing went great, but I'm so happy to finally be back home with Brian and Ella. I flick on the lights in the kitchen and I'm shocked to find the house is in pretty good shape. Just a few dirty dishes in the sink and a few toys scattered about in the living room. I half expected to come home to food on the walls, toys everywhere, and Lola and Ella eating out of Lola's food dish, while Brian laid on the floor in the fetal position, but it looks like he did great with his first full day alone with Ella.

Walking upstairs, I call out for Brian and Ella, but I'm met with silence. I check Ella's room but there is no sign of them. I stop at the doorway of our bedroom when I spot my little family inside, fast asleep. Brian has Ella sleeping on his chest, and Lola is curled up next to Brian. My heart warms at the sight. Three years ago, I never thought I would get my happy beginning. I felt so lost and numb after Jake died, but then the universe opened up and brought me a beautiful daughter and the most amazing man any woman could ever ask for. I finally feel like this is where I'm supposed to be.

I slip off my heels and climb under the covers. Just then Brian's eyes flutter open, and a relieved sleepy smile tugs at his lips. "Hi," he says with a sleepy sigh.

"Hi, I see you guys survived without me." I smile, lean in and kiss Brian then softly kiss the top of Ella's head and rub her back.

"Told you I got this." Brian confidently grins.

"I can see that, but I bet you'll be happy to get back to running down bank robbers and drug dealers tomorrow," I tease.

"Oh hell yes. I love Ella but she is a handful. I have a whole new respect for everything you do around here. So how was the signing?" he asks with a yawn.

"It went great, but I'm glad to be home with you guys. You did a wonderful job with Ella today, Brian. You are such a good daddy. I hope you know that."

"I'm realizing it more and more thanks to you." He softly smiles, tilting his head up to kiss me. I love this man so damn much.

"Why don't I go get Ella her bottle, and it looks like daddy could definitely use his own bottle too," I say, hiding a giggle. "Then we can have a picnic in bed and watch movies."

"That sounds perfect."

ACKNOWLEDGEMENTS

TO MY AMAZING BETA READERS, Kellie, Laurie and Taylor, thank you for all of your encouragement, support and most importantly your honesty. You ladies keep me sane when I want to throw in the towel. I love you girls to the moon and back.

To my biggest cheer squad, my IG crew, Bookmarkbelles, Booknerdingout, innergoddess_booklover, lovekellankyle, Taylors_pages, Laurie, Giovanna, Amanda, Kinkygirlsbookobsessions and rentasticreads. Thank you for everything you do for me, from making teasers to sharing my books. You girls are freaking rock stars!

And last but not least, to my husband, thank you for supporting me and my crazy dream. You are the love of my life and I love you more every single day.

MORE BOOKS BY M. ANDREWS

The Big Gamble—Gambling on Love Book 1

Lucky Strike—Gambling on Love Book 2

Taking Chances—Hot Hollywood Nights Book 1

Cupcake—Sticky Sweet Series Book 1

Sweet Seduction—Sticky Sweet Series Book 2

COMING SOON

Add to you TBR on Goodreads

Partners in Crime—Gambling on Love Book 3

Queen of Hearts—Gambling on Love Book 4

Sweetest Wedding—Sticky Sweet Series Book 3

ABOUT THE AUTHOR

M. ANDREWS RESIDES IN THE suburbs of Seattle with her family. She is a self-proclaimed cupcake hound and coffee addict who loves to write sticky sweet erotic romance.

Connect with me online

Facebook

Goodreads

Instagram

Made in the USA
Coppell, TX
10 December 2022